HEART OF

P. JAMESON

P. Jameson

HEART OF GOLD

P. Jameson
www.pjamesonbooks.com

Published in the United States of America

First Digital Publication: May 2017
First Print Publication:

Formatting and Cover Design: Agent X

Cover Model: Shade Moran

Photography by Furious Fotog

DEDICATION

For all the people looking for the bright spots in
the midst of darkness.

ACKNOWLEDGEMENTS

Once again, the hugest thanks to my team of people behind the scenes. Without them, these books would never see the light of day. Editing, formatting, cover photography and design, cheerleading me on when I'm losing my confidence. Y'all... there are so many arms to the PJ machine, and I love and appreciate them all.

Thank you to my family. My Mr. PJ and my little monsters. They allow me to follow this passion with everything in me, knowing that I always come back to them. They're never far from my mind even when I'm locked in my office tackling a sick deadline. They have my whole heart. Even the little pieces I leave in the books.

And finally, thank you, readers. I can never say it enough. You have believed in me from the beginning and loved so many characters along with me, and it means more than I have words for. Here's to many more years together!

One

It started as a whisper. As all important moments in life do.

Her.

So softly, it crept from deep within his soul. His mangled, vicious soul. Whatever of it was left.

Her. Her, her.

It grew louder. More urgent. Uncomfortable.

Thomas "Ratchet" Golding stared down at the female curled into the tightest ball on the floor of the storage shed behind a row of trash barrels, wondering if she was dead.

No. Not dead. Too pink to be dead. But definitely asleep. Which seemed all wrong since he'd just tromped his way in here without a care.

Carefully, he crouched low to investigate. Her dark hair was snarled all to hell. Like she'd rolled around on a Velcro pillow. Some of it hung over her dirty face, but he didn't dare touch her to move it. A thin hooded jacket was all she had for warmth, and the boots on her feet had a tear on the toe of the left one. The nails of both hands were broken. Several were caked with dried blood. Knuckles were bruised. Lips were cracked. And he suspected other parts of her were just as damaged even though they were covered by her clothes.

Her. She's the one. Keep her.

Ratchet frowned at the voice whispering through his head. It was foreign. New. But similar to the voice he'd heard his whole life until two years ago. The one that belonged to his inner cat. His lion.

The lion he couldn't call from his body

anymore.

The one who'd hurt so many.

The one who had no voice anymore, no instinct to guide Ratchet. The one he'd relied on his entire life.

The one that *failed* him.

The cat would be able to hear her heartbeat, her breathing. The cat could be sure of her status. It would scent her, and know where she'd been. Who she'd been with. Whether she was dosed…

But without the cat, Ratchet couldn't know any of those things.

Locked inside his body because of a curse, the animal had faded to something else. Something quiet. Something hardly there. Something learning. Changing.

The female whimpered in her sleep, assuring Ratchet that she was indeed alive. She jerked, her hands curling into claws, and for a breath, he thought she was awake. But she'd moved enough to shake the hair from over her eyes, and he could see she was still out. Deep in a nightmare, if her whispered, "no, no," was anything to go by.

Should he wake her?

He glanced around, listening for any sign of the others. He didn't call any of them brother anymore. They weren't that. Not a brotherhood like they'd once been, brought together for the sole purpose of hurting others to gain power. The goal was to have so much of it, nothing stopped them from getting what they wanted, whatever that might be. No life was worth more than power. That had been the motto ground into them from a young age.

Now they were a miserable bunch of damaged shifters that had nowhere else to go. They were as any other human, but worse off. Because at least humans didn't know what they were missing. The power of a shift, your body changing from one form to another at your beck and call. The power of the fear it instilled in others when your beast could overtake them with barely any effort.

Ratchet had lived off that fear.

Hungered for it.

The eyes pulled wide to see all the whites. The terror in a scream... he'd bathed in that, lapped it up like fucking cream.

Now he didn't give one shit about making anyone piss their pants. He'd trade every piece of the past to have his animal back to working. One half of everything he was, just gone, in a blink... yeah, he'd do it all again differently if he had a chance.

They all would.

Everyone except Felix. The leader of their clan wasn't so easily swayed by a little suffering. He'd been raised on worse. And something told Ratchet, the male was just biding his time until he could find a way out of his human shell. If it ever happened, the world was going to see what a were-jag rampage looked like. Ratchet had seen enough human Felix rampages to know an animal one wouldn't be pretty.

"No, no," the female murmured louder. Her voice was small and fragile, but it made noise.

And noise would attract the others.

Others included Felix.

And Felix might hurt her.

Which was unacceptable.

Ratchet frowned. Why would he care? He didn't know this female, and she was trespassing on private property.

Because it's her. *Yours.*

His? Bullshit. His mind was messing with him. Telling him things that might make him keep trying, when all he wanted to do was stop.

Stop going. Stop working.

Stop living, because he wasn't really living anyway, and hadn't been for a long, long time. Even before the battle that left him and the others crippled.

Besides, he didn't believe the Alley Cats were getting fixed like some of them did. Skittles, that hopeful bastard, liked to think there was a way out, and Felix urged him on, if only so that one day he could get his revenge.

Ratchet wasn't that stupid.

The abominable didn't get happily-ever-afters. They got hellfire and brimstone.

"No!" The female's terrified cry rattled through the storage shed, making Ratchet stiffen. Her eyes popped open, going wide in emerald terror. The green irises, rimmed in red-streaked whites, was a testament to whatever she'd been dreaming. They zeroed in on him and went impossibly wider.

She jerked to a sit, scrambling backward and slamming into an empty barrel. The metal sliding against the concrete made an ear-splitting noise that was sure to grab anyone's attention if they were near.

Shit.

Ratchet lunged forward to grab her, but she kicked her foot out just as he was about to connect. Her booted heel hit him just underneath the ribs, stealing his breath like a punch. She tried to crawl away, but couldn't get very far, trapped by the barrels like she was. With a growl, he came at her side ways, reaching, but she knocked his hands away with a whimper. Her head went side to side. "No, no, please," she begged, and it hit his chest all wrong.

He liked begging. Begging meant he was in control and the other person could be crushed under his toe like a tiny ant. Begging meant he had all the power. Begging was sweet music to his ears.

But not now.

Now it twisted his heart up like a crumpled sheet of paper in an angry fist.

"The hell is that?" Felix's voice boomed across the parking lot outside.

"Whatever," Skittles said in his normal bored tone. "Someone rummaging through the shed."

"Don't sound like someone rummaging. Sounds like someone messing shit up."

"Ain't nothing to mess up," Skittles argued. "Just some old barrels and tools. We sold off all the valuables."

The female started up again. "Please, please, please..."

"Shhh," Ratchet hurried out, but he knew it was too late.

"Did you hear that?" Felix said darkly.

"Hear what?"

Footsteps crunched heavily through the gravel, getting closer and closer. And something crazy happened.

Ratchet felt fear.

Deep inside, way down.

So far down, he wondered if had ever existed at all. But he knew it did. It had just been beaten out of him at a young age. It was the only way to make an Alley Cat. Form them through careful intimidation, physical pain, emotional pain, and give them zero to live for except power. Always about the power.

But his fear wasn't for himself. He'd been hoping Felix would cut him down for good for a while now. No. His fear was for the terrified little female who'd chosen their storage shed floor for a bed. He knew what Felix did to females. What they all did. Physically, none had been harmed.

Mentally, he couldn't say the same.

His stomach curled as the memories of his sins rose like cream to the top. The lying, the stealing, the using.

He was a bastard. They were all bastards.

He couldn't let this female fall victim. He couldn't change what he'd done in the past, but he could damn well keep another human from experiencing that shit. Maybe it would be his grand finale. Save her and then leave, like Gash did, like Malcom did.

Except leave permanently. Just stop... being.

"Ple—"

In a smooth move, Ratchet jerked her up off the floor and slid his hand over her mouth to muffle her pleas. Her back to his front, he locked her in with his forearm and tightened it until she stopped struggling.

"Hush, woman. Someone worse than me is coming." The smash of boots was nearly at the door.

He could tell her to run. Leave here and stay

away. But what if Felix found her on the way out? What if she was stupid and came back? What if whatever she was scared of caught her... and was worse than Felix?

Keep her, the voice inside whispered.

There was only one thing to do.

Ratchet dragged her past the barrels and out the back door of the storage shed, just as Felix and Skittles strolled in the front.

Two

It was a dream. She was dreaming of course. She'd done it so many times before. Terrible dreams of being captured—the way she had been in real life. Tortured. Harmed. But they always ended with her escape. And if not her escape, then death. Which she was starting to see as a type of escape.

A dream. A nightmare. That was all.

She just had to get through this one, like all the others, and when she woke up, she'd be on her way. She needed to get farther. Hopefully out of

Memphis. Possibly to the other side of the country.

Despair licked her. Was there a place far enough away from her captor?

Former captor, she reminded herself.

The man from the shed handled her gruffly as they moved in the shadows of the parking lot. Maybe she could make her escape now. This dream was different than her others. She'd never had this chance before. But they were nearing a door. Once inside, her chance would be over, she knew.

She squeezed her eyes closed, reciting the words that had become her lifeline over the years.

Your name is Marlee Benson.

You are twenty-eight years old.

You had a dog named Jem.

You were last free on your eighteenth birthday.

You were in the news. Someone will find you.

Don't forget. Don't forget. Don't forget.

Opening her eyes, she found the door. It was closer than she expected. Now. She had to try now.

Using her bony elbow as her best weapon, she rammed it into the man's ribs while jerking forward at the same time, kicking to get loose. But he barely grunted in response, and tightened his hold to death grip status. She let out a desperate shriek through his fingers where they clamped onto her mouth, and he pulled her into a cove between a wall and a dumpster.

"Stop it, ya hear?" he growled into her ear. His stern voice sent a warning down her spine. "I promise, I will keep you safe. I won't hurt you and I won't let anyone else hurt you either. But you have to be quiet. If he finds you, we're both fucked."

He. The monster was here? But of course he was. This was her nightmare. The one she fought through every night.

Despair made her go limp against the strange man. She was defeated now, by her subconscious. But when she woke, she would run again. Run until she was lost. Until she was strong again.

She hoped she could be strong again.

"Now, let's get inside. We see anyone, you keep your head down. Got it? Don't look anyone in the eye. Nod if you understand."

She moved her head and hope it was something like a nod.

It must have been enough, because he angled her out of the cove and toward the door. When they slipped through, he pulled his hand from her mouth, but not before pulling her chin up so her eyes met his warning glare. He was a beautiful man with a rough looking snarl to his lips. Eyes that were deceptively blue like a summer sky, but didn't contain a hint of any of that happiness. Blond hair that dipped to his shoulders and hung in his face in straggled pieces.

But his message was clear. If she made a sound, she'd be in trouble.

He turned his head, looking left then right. They were in some sort of warehouse. Boxes and crates were piled along one wall and several sectioned office spaces took up another. Steel beams above her head supported a second floor, and she could hear angry music and snarled voices coming from there.

The man grabbed her arm, pulling her toward a rickety looking industrial staircase. She followed him up, tripping over the last step. He righted her before pulling her in close. She went rigid.

Too close. Don't want to be this close.

"It's okay," he whispered. "Just need to get past the lounge. Then we're home free."

They went down a dark corridor, the music and voices growing louder with each step, and she kept her head down just like he'd instructed. Even though they stuck to the wall of the lounge, it felt like they were right in the middle of a pit of vipers. She heard men and women. Cursing and grunting. Laughing and snarling. Bottles clanking. Chairs squeaking. She didn't even want to know what happened in the lounge.

She felt the exit nearing when a slurring voice stopped them. "Who-ya got there, Ratchet?"

Luckily it didn't stop all the others. The room still vibrated with noise.

The man's grip on her tightened before it relaxed and he wound both arms around her like they were familiar. He pressed her into his chest and she narrowly resisted the urge to struggle. Bile rose in her throat.

He was strong like her captor. Tall like her captor. Never ending like her captor.

She managed to draw in a ragged breath and somehow it was exactly what she needed to keep from screaming.

He didn't smell like her captor. Like sweat and expensive cologne and stale cigars.

No. This man smelled natural. Like grass and the air beside a creek. Something fresh. New.

"None of your business," he rumbled to answer the slurred question.

The stranger grunted. "Fine. You gonna fuck 'er? Wanna share?"

"Fuck off, Fang," her new captor snapped. "I don't share, and you know it."

"Well, shit. Fine. Can't blame a guy for trying."

Something that sounded like a hiss hit her ears and then they were moving again. The floor was concrete, dirty and cold. But when they reached a new room, there was a large brown rug. Strangely fluffy for a place like the warehouse. It somehow put her more at ease, if only for a moment.

The hands were gone from her and a door slamming made her jump. The sound of a lock engaging made her stomach go queasy. A lock meant she was trapped.

Carefully, she eased her gaze upward. She found his feet first. A pair of black construction boots that had seen better days. Then his legs. Jean clad. Muscular and long. She skipped over his waist and moved to his chest. He was broad. Big arms. He could overpower her easily. Already had. But the realization settled in, that he could do whatever he wanted to her, and there'd be no stopping him.

It was sheer terror in her veins.

Her panicked breaths came sharp and fast, a gasping staccato she couldn't stop. Tears beat at her eyelids as her gaze finally landed on his cruel one.

He was going to hurt her.

Nausea doubled her over as she wrapped her arms around her middle.

After so many years, she was surprised she could still cry at all. Was it the combination of being free, but always locked in these torturous dreams? Like she'd taken a piece of her captivity with her.

I'll never let you go. You can never escape, my doll, because I'm already right here, her captor had said, tapping one gnarly finger against her temple. Maybe he was right. Maybe what she'd been through could never be cleansed from her mind.

"You going to hurl?" the stranger asked.

Did he have a name? The man in the lounge called him something... Racket? Should she remember it? Or just forget. Fade out now, before she started feeling pain. Go to that place inside her that she escaped to when it got bad.

Her stomach heaved, but there wasn't anything in it to toss.

"Shit," he muttered, stepping around her and then returning with a wastebasket.

He shoved it under her face just as her middle clenched again. To her surprise something did come up. Bile and stomach acid and the little bit of water she'd been given just before escaping.

"What are you on?" he asked.

She spit into the trash can, coughing and sputtering out, "on?"

"You an addict? Or did someone slip you something?"

She frowned, hugging the can close, just in case. She shook so bad she wondered if she would be able to keep her feet under her.

"Not..." she breathed deep, trying to make her voice work. "Not an addict. Clean now."

"Bullshit." The words left his lips simply. Not angry. Not frustrated.

"C-clean as I could be. I only took what I was

given."

"What was it?"

"Don't know. Something in my water. But I..." Should she tell him this part? "I built up a tolerance. Started faking the effects so he wouldn't up my dose."

The stranger frowned so hard his forehead rippled like a stone in water. "How long?"

"H-how long what?"

"Since your last dose."

"I don't know... I... don't know."

The stranger came closer, invading her space like he could get the answers from just being near. Like they'd jump from her skin to his and crawl into his brain.

"Was it yesterday? Morning, afternoon? You must remember something. Lunch or dinner?"

Something ominous swept over her. This was all wrong. No one in her nightmares asked questions. They just took. Stole. Hurt. Crippled.

Blinking, she tried to understand the warning boulder that settled in the pit of her stomach. Her instincts, once pristine and honed, were trying to tell her something.

"What day is it?"

"Monday."

Her dreams never had time. They just were. No day, no hour. No AM or PM.

Fear was clawing her to shreds inside, because... this was starting to feel *real*. The stranger, the warehouse, the way he talked to her. None of it had that fuzzy quality she'd learned to rely on.

And... if this wasn't a dream, it meant... she was a captive. Again. It meant she had only escaped, to be really and truly captured again by someone else.

"No," she whispered, letting despair rip her apart.

There was no dream to wake from. There was no getting farther away from Memphis. Getting away from her captor. They'd only changed faces.

"*No.*" She shook her head, squeezing her eyes closed and praying when she opened them, she'd be somewhere else. Anywhere else but in a locked room she couldn't escape from.

But when she chanced it, the cruel blond stranger was even closer. Nearly touching her.

Too close, too close.

It was too much. Something inside snapped, broke in a way she desperately needed.

And her world went black.

Three

Ratchet watched the female collapse in slow motion. Like a skyscraper being demolished. Lunging forward, he managed to catch her just before she faceplanted on the floor.

"Shit."

She was small. Weighed practically nothing. Cradling her body in one arm, he knelt, tipping her head back to see her face.

Like this, she looked completely different. At peace again. The way she'd been when he first found her in the shed. No fear, no panic. No haunted shadows and shakes.

He let his gaze linger, taking in her features. Small forehead, large eyes rimmed in long lashes. A narrow nose that came to a point above bow-shaped lips. Delicate jaw. He was no authority on beauty. Didn't much care what women looked like. Or hadn't for a long time. But he could see this female was quite pretty under all the dirt.

His heart pounded in his chest. Leftover adrenaline from narrowly avoiding Felix in the shed and chancing bringing her inside where the others could see her. Thankfully, Fang was too drunk to be pushy. He'd let it go before catching anyone else's attention.

Ratchet ground his molars until his jaw cracked.

He would have fought him, he realized. He would've fought Fang off to keep this woman safe. Would've been beat to hell for it, but at least he would have gone down fighting.

Luckily it hadn't come to that. And now he had to be smart about this. The Alley Cats had relied on muscle and intimidation for so long. That's how they'd been outsmarted by a curse two years ago. And now Ratchet was going to outsmart them until his female could be safe.

He brushed her hair back. It was cut crooked. Chunky, like it had been hacked at with a knife. Curving his palm around one cheek awkwardly, he patted it, trying to stir her.

"Hey," he whispered. "Wake up, woman."

But she didn't respond.

He shook her harder.

"Come on. Need you to wake up."

He was ninety nine percent sure she was detoxing from whatever she'd been given. Something she'd been given repeatedly, if what she'd told him was true. He needed to get some water in her. Clean her up a little. Let her sleep so her body could get used to being without the drug. He'd put her in his bed and watch over her.

But he remembered the way she'd stiffened in the lounge when he pretended they were together. She didn't like being touched.

The realization turned to sadness in his veins.

Touch was the one thing that had anchored him throughout his life. He'd had it different than the others. A little. He had a mama that fought to stick around through all the bullshit the clan put them through. She hadn't left like so many others had. Or blotted out reality with alcohol and downers. Or turned a blind eye to the abuses of their leader before Felix. She'd known her place, known she couldn't stop what they'd turn her son into. But... for every fist Ratchet took, for every lash on his back, there was a soft touch from her. Like she'd hoped the one could balance out the other.

She was wrong, but at least she had tried.

She was human and soft. But for once, that didn't seem like a bad thing.

He stared down at the female in his arms, weighing out his next decision. Her shoulders were thin and felt frail. Her skin was pale and gray-tinged. *Malnourished*, the voice inside him murmured. She needed help. More help than he could give her.

Rising, he carried her to the bed and put her down on his pillow. He unlaced her boots and eased them from her feet, finding them bare underneath. And bloodied like her fingers.

Little thing, what happened to you?

Something fiercely protective came over him. A burning in his gut that made him hot from the inside. It was righteous anger and sympathy and territorial instinct all rolled into one flaming emotion behind the cage of his ribs.

A feeling he wasn't used to. And didn't fucking like.

But also… felt necessary.

It was powerful. In the way his cat used to be. Except it didn't feel sick like his lion did.

Carefully, he tucked the thick blanket around her, and stepped back to pull his cell phone from his pocket. He touched the button that would dial a familiar number. He could go downstairs and find who he was looking for, but he wouldn't chance leaving the female alone.

The phone rang twice in his ear before it clicked through.

"Mom," he cut out before she could say anything. "I need your help."

***

Leah Golding was used to the shifters needing her. Especially in recent years since their animals were locked inside.

When she was young and the world seemed bright, she'd fallen for a bad man. He'd fallen for her too, but no female came between him and his clan.

Brothers above all. Loyalty above all.

Leaving hadn't been an option. The son he gave her, belonged to the clan. And she wasn't giving her kid up. She wasn't leaving her innocent baby to the monsters. So she'd done the only thing a desperate mom could do.

She got smart. Got tough.

Became one of the clan so she could hold her son after the harsh lessons he was taught to prepare for his future as an Alley Cat. She'd spread her love out to all the children, hoping it'd make a difference somehow.

But looking at how they'd ended up... she realized it hadn't.

They'd all die early just like their fathers. Too many enemies. And no way to fight them.

She swallowed back her fear, the nasty lump in her throat, the ache of failing her only born and the ones she'd adopted into her heart.

Mom, I need your help.

Thomas needed her now.

She'd watched him spiral down, down, down helpless to change any of it. Over the years, all she could do was offer her love, and damn it, she believed in the power of love. But somehow it had never been enough.

If he was asking for her now, it was important.

Climbing the stairs from the office to the second floor, she grit her teeth at the booming music coming from the lounge. It was dark outside, so the party was in full swing. If you could call it that. The clan's nightly ritual of booze and babes. A Forget Shit Party. Couldn't solve their problems, couldn't live with being assholes with no animal to justify it, so their answer was to drink through their money.

She'd told Felix their holdings were depleting. He didn't seem to care. Or couldn't maybe. He was sicker than all the others. As if his human was so weak it was literally nothing without the jaguar. Pale, gaunt, with a broken gaze. The only hint of the dangerous man he used to be, was his mouth. He could still cut deep with that weapon.

And his heart. Still black, even cut in half.

Straightening her shoulders, she pushed into the lounge, studiously ignoring the people in half state of dress. The ones stumbling drunk. The ones humping in a corner. Her son's room was in the hall past the common area. She was almost there.

"Mama Kitty!" A slurred voice rose above the noise. It was what the boys called her. Half in affection, half in derision. Mama, like an endearment. Kitty to remind her she was human and lower than them.

Or... had been lower.

They were even now. More even than they cared to admit.

She looked up to find Fang and Monster lurching in her direction.

"Coming to party with us this time?" Fang asked while Monster tipped a bottle of Jack completely upside down into his mouth.

She gave them her easy smile. The one she'd perfected over the years to replace her real one. "Not this time, boys."

"Aw, hellllllll," Monster groused. "You say that every time though."

She planted one hand on her hip and cocked an eyebrow at the couple humping in the corner. "You really want an old lady bustin' your balls tonight? You know how I feel about what you boys do up here."

Monster gave her a toothy grin. His face was scarred all to hell, but he sure had a winning smile. It reminded her of how he was as a young. Happy as a child is, even if their life is shit. Before he'd been broken like a mare to do the clan's bidding. It always took a little while for that innocence to fade. She'd watched it happen too many times. Taking the soft, workable putty heart of a kid, smashing it with brutal hands until it resembled something grotesque, and hardening it with fire until it couldn't be molded into anything else.

Over the years, there had been more young born to the clan. So many women, just like her, with bleeding hearts for the bad boys. Bred, to keep the clan growing.

But she'd managed to get them—and their half-breed babies—all into hiding without the clan realizing it.

Sooooo many runaways. What a shame. That's what she'd told Felix. Commiserated with him over their losses. But even if she'd been caught, saving *any* would have been worth it.

There would be so many more young lives for

the Cats to ruin if it weren't for her.

"Now, Mama..." Monster drawled. "You ain't old. You're maybe an eight on the MILF scale."

"Yeah, I'd do ya," Fang agreed, swaying on his feet.

She rolled her eyes. "I'm honored, really. But no thanks. Your dick is like Forrest Gump, it's been everywhere."

"Got a point there," Monster agreed.

Fang smirked, belched. "I'm not seeing it as a bad thing."

They tried to bump fists and missed, shrugging it off and clearing their throats.

"Yeah, yeah. Alright, boys. I'm outta here. Reminder though: if you toss your cookies in the hall, I'm not cleaning it up."

She pushed past them, and got three steps before a sharp, "Mama," stopped her. She shook off the chills that slid up her spine. This voice wasn't slurred. Wasn't five shades to the wind. Sometimes they were better when they were drunk. How fucking sad was that.

She twisted to find Felix, the clan's leader, near the stairs. Once power seeped from his pores like a sponge. He'd ruled with something worse than an iron fist. A razor claw, a savage heart. Now he was a mere shade of his former self, but he could still induce fear, if only residual. A memory of past brutalities.

His breath was heavy, like he'd run a marathon, and he swayed, pushing one palm into the wall to stay steady. But his steely eyes were clear. Sharp. Knowing.

He narrowed them at her. "You been messing around in the shed today?"

Leah frowned. "Do I look like a raccoon? Shed's full of trash. No reason for me to go digging in it."

"Not trash," Skittles argued, climbing the stairs behind him. His brightly colored tattoos had earned him the nickname. And Fang liked to "help" him out in the ladies department by telling girls they should *taste the rainbow*. "Trash *barrels*," he corrected. "We don't keep trash just lying around."

"Trash barrels that are no longer being used and could be dumped off. So... trash. And still, not a raccoon."

Felix sighed heavily. "Is that a no?"

"That's a no," she confirmed. And it was true mostly. She hadn't needed to use the shed for over a year now.

He and Skittles shared a look. Felix shook his head, grumbling, and stalked off toward the liquor. Skittles shrugged and went in the other direction, plopping down on a ratty leather couch.

She'd have to keep her ears open for whatever had put them on alert.

Pushing into the hall was a relief. Being around the shifters always felt like an axe could fall at any moment. She held her breath, faked her cool, waiting for shit to hit the fan.

Thirty years of that feeling. And she would spend the rest of her years feeling it too. It was her penance for bringing a child into the twisted Alley Cat world. It wasn't what she'd wanted for her life, but she didn't mind paying the cost too much because it was the way things should be.

The only way to right a wrong was to deal with the consequences. And she had wronged her son by having him. Even if she didn't realize it at the time.

She knocked on Thomas's door, anxious about what would be on the other side. She'd stitched him up more times than she could count. Bandaged wounds. Found him sick over the toilet, passed out on the floor, angry and punching the wall... what would it be today? What horror was he facing that he'd actually *asked* for her this time?

His hurried footsteps approached. Not stumbling. Not drunk. Okay.

The door opened a crack and his snarling face appeared. Her Thomas was handsome. He had her blond hair, and blue eyes. But damn, he had his father's demeanor. His father's mean-ass smirk. She imagined what he would have looked like if he'd been raised anywhere else. No permanent frown probably. No darkness under his eyes. No scars on his back.

"You alone?" he hissed.

"Of course."

The door slid open just enough for her to walk through.

The room was dark compared to the hall, and it took her eyes a few seconds to adjust. When they did, she scanned the room, trying to get some idea of what was wrong. Nothing was broken or out of place. She looked her son over. No broken skin, no new bruises or busted bones.

"Thomas, what is it? What do you need—" But her voice cut off as her gaze finally landed on the bed.

Tucked into the covers was a dark-haired female. What Leah could see of her was dirty and bruised. Specks of blood edged her mouth. Leah knew what caused that. Split lip. A smack when she got out of line. She was out cold. No movement at all.

Leah rushed forward, bending over the bed to

test the girl's pulse. It was strong, if a little fast.

Good. Okay.

She turned to find Thomas, watching her intently.

He was like the others. He had females under him all the time. She wasn't an idiot. She knew. But he never took them to his room. Never allowed them in his space. It was how she was able to stomach knowing he was just like the others. It was enough to know he was never going to *keep* a female. Never get her with child. Never give the clan another young.

But now... now there was one in his bed. Clearly hurt. Unconscious.

Horror filled Leah. Did he do this? Hurt this one?

"Thomas... what have you done?"

Somehow she found his eyes. They flashed with some emotion that looked eerily similar to hurt. He straightened his shoulders, set his jaw in that stubborn way that put him above her. Reminded her she was lower. Always lower, even though he needed her. They *all* needed her.

"She's mine. Fix her."

Four

"Did you do this?"

The question was like a slap in the face coming from her. Did she really think he'd hurt a female like this? Yeah, he'd had his share of women in his bed. In the lounge. Whatever.

Women who wanted to be used. But he'd never *taken* anything from anyone. Threatened a few times, to assert power when it was needed. He was an asshole for sure. But the girl in his bed had it worse than any of that. And it turned his stomach seeing her in such bad shape.

No. He didn't do this.

But he tried to remember why his mother might think so.

Their fathers had been this bad. The generation who ruled the Alley Cats before them.

"If I did, would I be trying to fix her?" he asked through tight teeth. "Would I have called you here?"

His mother pulled the covers back, messing up the careful way he'd tucked the girl in. Her gaze rolled over her fragile body. The ratted flannel jacket she wore. The jeans that were too big. Before she covered her back up.

"Why is she here?"

"I found her." He liked finding things. He found treasures in the trash he collected all the time. People threw away some of the most interesting things.

His mother gave him a skeptical look.

"Tell me what happened."

"I brought her up here to hide her from Felix. I was trying to get her damn name when she passed out. She's coming off something, pretty sure."

She pressed two fingers to the female's neck to check her pulse, and seemed to be counting.

"Is she okay?" Ratchet fidgeted, waiting for an answer. He wasn't patient on a normal day, and he definitely wasn't now.

"Pulse is fast. Any idea what she's on?"

He shook his head. "Something in her drink she said. Long term. Built up a tolerance to it."

His mother frowned. "A sedative then. Get me some water. She needs to drink. We'll get her cleaned up when she wakes. Get some food in her if she can keep it down."

Ratchet stomped over to the little fridge in the corner of his room. It was mostly full of beer, but there was some bottled water there too.

When he brought it back, he started to twist off the lid.

"No. Leave it. She'll want to see us open it."

He frowned. Why would she want to do that?

"Hey." His mother shook the female. Gently.

Like she used to do to wake him up. "Hey, sweetie. Can you open your eyes?"

The female moaned softly. Like the motion hurt. But his mother didn't stop shaking her. In fact, she went harder.

"Come on, hun. You need to wake up."

A whimper escaped but it turned into a twisted cry. The sound tied his stomach up in knots. He fisted his hands against the feeling.

"Shh." His mother brushed the female's hair with her fingers. "Wake up," she said gently. "Time to get some liquid in you."

His girl's eyelids flickered, those long lashes twitching to open but not quite pulling it off.

"There you go. Almost there. Open your eyes for me. It's okay."

This time she woke, her gaze foggy as it landed on his mother.

"Hi there. I'm Leah." She gave the female a friendly smile, but there was no hiding the edge in her expression. A well-concealed fear. His mother wore it always, he realized. If not in her look, then in her mannerisms. "I'm going to help you as best I can. We need to start by getting some fluids in you, okay?"

The female seemed confused and her gaze skittered around looking for anything familiar. But then they landed on Ratchet and went from confused to lucid in a blink.

"No, no, no..." she whimpered, scrambling to a sit too fast and almost knocking the water bottle out of his mother's hand. Terror creased the edges of her gaze and crimped her lips. "Y-You." She pointed a shaking finger at Ratchet and it felt like she was accusing him with it. "You don't touch me."

He frowned at her command. And inside, he stood at attention, the voice demanding he listen well. *Don't touch her.* Okay. He wouldn't.

It made him feel... sad. How could he help her if he couldn't touch her?

He found his mother's confused gaze. She probably thought he'd done something ugly. Why should she think any different? He was filled with that familiar shame even though he'd done nothing to the female. Always with the shame.

He swallowed hard, pushing it all down.

The female needed fixing. That was all that mattered.

Yes, murmured the voice.

Ratchet gave her a nod. "I won't lay a finger on you. But let my mother help you."

She switched her green gaze back to Leah, skeptical.

"You've been hurt," his mother said, "but it's going to be okay. We will get you stronger and get you out of here."

Ratchet's gaze snapped to his mother.

No. She can't leave. We've finally found *her*.

The new voice inside was panicking now, and he wasn't used to the feeling. Panic wasn't something an Alley Cat ever let show. You pushed the shit down. Always. Be. In. Control.

"Y-you'll let me go?"

Never.

His mother looked at him, clearly unsure of

the promise she'd made. "When it's safe. For now, drink."

The female was shaking her head back and forth so fast she was going to be dizzy if she wasn't already. "No water. Please. No water."

His mother's voice was calm. Like she knew exactly how to talk to the woman. "Ratchet tells me you were dosed. We aren't doing that to you. Look..." She held the sealed bottle out for the female to see. "Unopened. You can do it yourself. That way you know. It's just water."

She stared, unsure. Her gaze flicked to Ratchet and his stomach flopped. Her eyes on him felt good. Even with that edge of fear in them.

He'd make that go away though. Show her he was safe.

Not safe. Not yet, the voice argued.

He set his jaw and tried to make sure his eyes seemed dull. No reaction. Never show a reaction unless it's anger.

He tipped his chin toward the water, urging her wordlessly to drink. She reached for it, carefully, and when it was in her hand, she cradled it close to her chest. She breathed hard, staring between Ratchet and his mother.

With trembling fingers, she attempted to unscrew the plastic cap. The blood and dirt caked under her nails turned the lid grimy. And she winced, not able to break the seal. She tried again, gritting her teeth.

"What happened to your fingers?" he growled. The boom of his voice froze her.

Too hard. Too loud.

"How did you hurt your fingers?" he tried, softer. He wasn't good at soft shit.

"Scraping," she murmured. "To... to get the window open. And then climbing the fence. It was wooden. And tall."

She'd hurt herself escaping. But from where? From whom?

Ratchet pushed the questions aside. Swallowed down the bile that came with the knowledge his female had endured something awful.

And that maybe the awful shit wasn't over for her yet. She'd landed in Alley Cat territory. Nothing good could come of that.

He didn't touch her, but he reached his hand forward. "I can open it for you."

She pressed her lips together and instead, held the bottle out to his mother to open.

Ratchet cleared his throat, crossing his arms and staring at the floor to hide his disappointment while the female drank.

"Slow down, hun. Don't want you to get sick. Sip it down, okay?"

He found her again as she was pulling the bottle from her mouth. The tremors were so bad she sloshed some over the edge.

"What's your name?" his mother asked.

"I'm Thirteen—" She shook her head. "No. My name is Marlee."

Marlee.

Her name made the voice inside go still. Made everything inside just... calm.

Marlee. *Her.*

He wanted to say it out loud and feel it on his lips.

He mouthed it silently instead. Later he would whisper it. Get his mouth familiar with it so she wouldn't flinch when he spoke it for the first time.

"What's Thirteen?" his mother asked, helping Marlee drink some more.

"It's what he called me. He has five dolls. He used to have more. We don't have names. Only numbers. I was unlucky number thirteen. But I don't forget."

"Don't forget what, hun?" His mother's voice was choked thin, but calm. Why did it seem like she'd done this before? Like she was a veteran at calming down scared females. At digging information out of them.

"Who I am," Marlee said bravely, her chin jutting so slightly it was barely noticeable.

Ratchet noticed.

"My name is Marlee Benson. I am twenty-eight years old. I had a dog named Jem. I was last

HEART OF GOLD

free on my eighteenth birthday. I was in the news. Someone will find me. Don't forget. Don't forget. Don't forget."

It was a mantra. She recited it with her eyes closed. Like she was trying to remember. Like she'd whispered it a million times to herself. Like it was the thing that kept her going through whatever darkness she'd endured.

Marlee Benson.

The female had been in captivity for ten years, if she was right about the details. Stripped of her identity... the same way Ratchet was stripped of his. Of his animal. And treated so poorly she could barely keep down her water.

And now... she was captive again.

Ratchet pumped his fists wanting something to hurt on her behalf. He didn't understand these protective instincts, the way his heart seemed to be claiming her when it shouldn't be possible. When it was fucking dangerous to. Wanting revenge for someone other than himself, it wasn't normal.

"Okay, Marlee," his mother said. "That's good. You keep remembering that."

Her green gaze large and worried, she nodded, whispering, "I don't forget."

And it was all he could take.

Ratchet stalked to the door, escaping through it before he blew his top and scared her even more.

Fuck everything.

Five

Marlee flinched at the sharp bang of the door slamming shut. The man was frightening. But it wasn't just because of his size or the permanent snarl on his face or the hard way he talked. The most frightening thing was the way he stared at her. Like he knew her. Not just recognized her from the news or something. But... *knew* her. Inside her middle. Where nobody was allowed.

It made her feel strange. Scared, but curious. And curiosity was part of what made the last ten years hell. If only she hadn't asked for answers.

Why she was a prisoner. When could she leave…

She'd never make that mistake again.

"Don't pay him any mind," the woman murmured. "He left so he could be angry without scaring you."

Leah was her name, and she seemed nice. Marlee didn't trust people. Not anyone anymore. But her gut told her Leah was… *something*. Not safe, but wanted to be.

"How do you know?"

"He's my son. He doesn't handle emotion well. None of them do. And I can feel it rolling off him like a tidal wave."

None of them do. That reminded her there were more. More men, drunk and doing unspeakable things if the sounds she'd heard in the lounge were anything to go by.

She had to get out of here.

"He'll be back?"

Leah nodded.

"Then I should go now. Can you help me get out of here? I need to be out of Memphis by tonight. Gotta get far away. People are looking for me. *His* people. And they always find what they're looking for."

"Your captor's people?" Leah asked.

"Yes. Please."

"Do you know his name?"

Marlee nodded, but she wasn't telling yet. He was too well-known. Too powerful.

"Where am I?"

Leah glanced at the door, looking unsure. She'd called the man Ratchet. And he'd called her mother.

"Alley Cat headquarters," she admitted finally. "It's not safe here, but my son won't let you be hurt. I have to believe that. And it's not possible for you to leave yet. No one knows you're here but me and him. If the others find out..."

Alley Cats. She'd heard the name from her captor. *Former captor.* They worked for him, if she could be sure of the conversations she'd heard.

Her stomach lurched.

Once they found out she belonged to him,

they'd return her.

She wrapped her arms around her middle, desperately trying to hold in her new panic. She felt like the bottom was falling out of her soul, everything just sinking... sliding... crashing.

"We... we could call the police," she whispered in desperation. "Tell them who I am."

Leah's face turned from careful to hard. "No police. They can't help you here."

More sinking-gut feeling as it occurred to her what she already knew. The police wouldn't lift a finger against her former captor, why would they do anything for her new ones. His *employees.*

"Only I can help you, but I can't do it right now," Leah hissed. "And until I can, you have to survive. Understand me? You stay here, in this room. Do what you're told until I can get you free."

"What I'm told?"

"Thomas won't hurt you." But she didn't sound one hundred percent on that.

"Thomas?"

"Ratchet. They call him Ratchet. And his

heart... it's fair. Not good, but fair. Deep down, he knows how to be right. He just needs to remember. Now, he brought you here to keep you safe. I have to believe that means something. Trust him, and no one else. Got it?"

Marlee remembered what he'd told her in the shed and when he'd dragged her into the warehouse. *I won't hurt you and I won't let anyone else hurt you either.*

How could she trust him? How could she trust anyone?

"Tell me you'll do what I say," Leah demanded, squeezing her hand. The desperation in the woman's gaze felt identical to hers. Was she captive too? Was she in as much danger as Marlee was?

Trust him, and no one else.

Damn it. Did she have a choice? Did she *ever* have a choice.

No. Never.

The day she had a choice would be the day she was finally *actually* free.

Until then, it was the same as it had been for ten years. Survive.

She nodded, feeling sicker than when she first awoke in the shed.

Leah let out a relieved breath. "Okay. Let's get you cleaned up and more comfortable. It's going to be all right, Marlee. I promise."

But promises meant nothing to a captive.

**

Ratchet paced the hallway outside his room. He'd been heading to the lounge for a drink but couldn't go more than six steps before turning back. Now he was repeating the action, trying to work out this fucked up situation in his mind.

He needed more information.

Like who was responsible for Marlee's condition? Because he was going to fuck them up good. If he had his cat still, he'd call it out and eat the bastard's goddamn face.

Or where was she kept? Because he was going to raze it to the ground. Burn it down and let her watch so she knew she'd never have to go back there.

Or what was done to her... because he needed to undo it all. Somehow.

He ran a shaking hand through his hair. What the fuck was happening to him? The need to care for this stranger was nearly overwhelming. It made his center burn to the point of being uncomfortable. Like whatever was inside him now was forcing him to action.

Do something. Make her better, and she will make you better. She can heal you where you're broken. It's her. The one.

Ratchet frowned. He couldn't be healed. He was shattered. No one would ever be able to find all the shards much less put them all back in their place.

You'll see. One thing at a time.

What could he do for her right now?

Tearing out the hearts of her enemies would have to come later, when he'd collected more intel.

Ratchet stared at the closed door, thinking.

She needed food. His female needed food. He'd hunt some down.

This got his feet moving toward the lounge. There was always food around when a party was happening. And when he got there, he wasn't disappointed. Past the people humping in dark corners and some shamelessly on the couches, he found tonight's buffet spread out over the counter. It wasn't even picked over yet. The empty beer and liquor bottles littering the floor told him most of the cats had skipped dinner and gone straight for the numbing agents.

Ratchet skipped the stack of paper plates, and dug around in the cabinet for a tray instead. He found a banged up cookie sheet. It would do.

Moving down the counter, he picked out the best looking sandwich. It looked like turkey probably, and the lettuce was nice and green. He grabbed several slices of pizza for Marlee to choose from, not knowing which kind his female would like. He passed on the chips. They looked stale. Fucking Fang had probably left the bag open again.

Ratchet stepped back, looking the food over. None of this shit was healthy. It wouldn't be good for her, but at least it would fill her empty stomach.

Again, the vice around his heart tightened at the thought of some asshole withholding food from her. Making her fear even water.

He found the chocolate cake off to the side. It looked like the kind his mom made. There was still three pieces left. Which told him the guys were worse off tonight than usual.

Ratchet slid all three pieces onto the tray and several chocolate chip cookies before digging in the fridge for something other than beer for Marlee to drink. He stared at the half-empty carton of milk wondering how many of the guys had swigged right from the jug. Nasty bastards.

Tucked away in the back there was an unopened bottle of orange juice. Perfect.

Turning to leave, he caught Skittles eyeing him from across the room. The cat was leaned against the wall, one leg drawn up to look casual, sipping from a bottle of Corona. He looked suspicious as all hell, and Ratchet was going to have to pass him on the way back into the hall.

He straightened his shoulders, setting his jaw as he went to stroll by like nothing at all was wrong. But Skittles stopped him with a whistle. Not an eerie one like their leader used right before he was about to fuck someone up. But a low, confused one.

"Lotta food you got there." Skittles' tone was quiet. He wasn't aiming to draw attention, but even if he was, the others were probably too far gone to notice. Or care. "Ain't seen you eat like that in a while."

Ratchet shrugged. "What do you care?"

Skittles narrowed his eyes, pushing off from the wall. "I don't. Just odd. Your ass has been skipping dinner for weeks."

"Guess it caught up with me."

"Yeah. Because that looks like enough food for two."

A snarl curled Ratchet's lips, warning his brother to back off. "Real hungry."

"Sure. Okay."

Pushing past Skittles, he started down the hall.

"It's just earlier we heard someone in the storage shed. But when we checked it out, no one was there. Only this."

Ratchet turned slowly, making sure his expression was neutral. Skittles pulled a worn photo from his back pocket and held it up. It must be Marlee's. She could have dropped it when Ratchet pulled her from the shed.

Shit.

His gut took a dive to the floor.

He reached for the thing, roughly pulling it from Skittles' grip, and stared closely at the images. Four unsmiling females in a dim room. Each with the same messy haircut and grim expression as Marlee. Different eyes and skin color, but the same hopelessness.

Four dolls. The fifth was in his room.

"Know anything about it?"

Ratchet pressed his lips together, shaking his head and passing the picture back to Skittles. "Nope."

"Fang said he saw you go in there earlier."

"Fang was drunk by noon. He probably saw little piggies dancing out in the lot too. Can't really depend on nothing he sees."

Skittles nodded, stuffing the photo back into his pocket.

"Try an alarm. Or hell, locking the door," Ratchet called over his shoulder as he forced himself to go slow down the hall. "Only way to keep things out of the damn shed is to lock it."

"Brilliant," Skittles deadpanned. "Fucking genius."

Ratchet flipped his middle finger high in the air and kept walking.

At his room, he eased the door open and slipped inside with the tray of food. There was a fleeting moment of despair when he noticed his bed was empty and neither his mother nor Marlee were anywhere to be seen. But then he heard their quiet voices coming from the small bathroom tucked at the back of the space and the air returned to his lungs.

With a frustrated sigh, he set the food on the dresser.

Why was his female out of bed? She should be resting.

The bathroom door was ajar and through it, he could see his mother helping a naked Marlee into the shower.

He froze, staring at her body. It was bruised and dirty, and she moved awkwardly. Like it wasn't her own. Or hadn't been for a long time. But her delicate shoulders, the curve of her spine, the soft sway of her waist... it called to him.

And felt wrong to look at.

Not wrong. Mine.

And besides, he looked at whatever he wanted. Women were meant to be looked at.

So why did he feel like king dick looking at her in this vulnerable moment?

Suddenly, Marlee's eyes shot across the bathroom as if she'd sensed him watching. She gasped, looking somehow betrayed, and he jerked his gaze away, pulling the door shut until it clicked.

Shit.

He listened for the water to change, the sound of the glass door sliding shut. And when he knew Marlee was safe inside, he resumed the pacing he'd done in the hallway, his small room only allowing him four good strides.

Whatever. He could pace all night if he needed. It was better than the miserable sleepless nights he'd grown used to.

Better than wanting an end to everything and wishing he'd been born to a different clan.

Yeah, the quarreling in his chest was confusing... but it was *something*. And until he got things straight, he wasn't checking out of life.

Six

The warm water burned as it poured from the spout over Marlee's skin. There were cuts and scrapes, but mostly it was just that her skin hurt. Her actual skin, bruised or not.

She'd been in the dark too long. And never enough nutrients because food costed money and put her more in debt to her captor.

Debts she was forced to work off.

Other girls had become accustomed to working for their food even though none of them had chosen to be there. Seemed like if you were going to kidnap a person, at least there should be some free food involved. Unless you were aiming to starve them to death. But her captor wanted them all alive. The answer: charge them for the food they ate, the clothes they wore, the toiletries they required.

Add it to the debt they were there to pay off in the first place. Add it to the mountain of unpaid bets or unpaid drug deals or unpaid... whatever.

For Marlee, none of that debt was hers. It belonged to her deadbeat father who couldn't stay away from the casinos. It had taken a year for her to understand why she was in the basement with the others in the first place.

The others.

She wondered if they were paying for her escape. She'd promised Seven... er, Nyla... she would give their picture to the authorities when she got far away from Memphis. But now it looked like that was going to take a lot longer than she'd ever anticipated. She hoped the girls didn't think she'd abandoned them like so many others had when they were freed.

Carefully, she forced more of her achy body under the warm spray, letting her skin get used to the harsh feeling. Since she refused to willingly "pay" her father's debt with her body and had no other skills to offer like the others, she wasn't allowed to shower like them. She'd bathed with water from the sink as best she could.

Her captor had made a bad bet of his own thinking Marlee's dad would care enough about her to pay the asshole the thousands he owed. She wondered where he was right now. David Benson. The sorry asshole who'd missed every one of her birthdays. Her graduation. And now ten more years of her life because she'd been locked away "serving time" for him.

She knew he wasn't alive. He'd died from a knife wound after spending the night in the county jail for drunk and disorderly. Her captor had told her that. Showed her the newspaper article.

But she wondered where he'd been buried.

She'd like to visit the grave and spit on it.

And if she could have a wish, it would be to know what he'd be doing *right now*, if he was alive.

Would he even wonder if she was still alive? If she'd survived. Would it ever cross his mind at all? Would he be sorry for stealing from a powerful man?

But honestly, did she even want to know the answers to those questions?

No. She didn't. Couldn't stomach it yet. Not until she was truly free and the others were too.

Her mom though… she wanted to know what had come of her mom.

Despair wracked her at the thought of the only person who ever gave a shit about her. What she must have gone through when Marlee went missing…

She'd seen her once on the news on the little TV in the basement. Crying and begging for Marlee's release. Even mentioned her captor's name. Called him out, right there on live television.

Marlee thought that was the end. That she would be found and rescued.

But nothing swayed him.

Money.

Money would have swayed him.

Grabbing the bar of green soap from the tile shelf, she lathered up the best she could, ignoring Leah as she stood with her back to the shower to give Marlee the most privacy she'd had in ten years.

Using the shower wall for support, she cleaned all the things that had been abandoned for so long and used the fresh razor Leah had found for her. She tried to ignore the tremors and focus on not cutting herself. But they were getting worse it seemed.

Drugs.

She never wanted so much as a damn aspirin ever again. She wanted clean of it all.

The memories. The truth. The pain.

Come on Marlee. Get clean in here, then sleep

off the shakes.

She could do it. As long as Leah was right about Ratchet. If she could trust him to let her be. And she wasn't sure she could after catching him watching from the doorway.

When she'd scrubbed and shaved as good as she could, she reached for the shampoo. It was in an amber colored bottle and looked expensive. Ratchet had long hair, but he didn't seem like the type who went for the pricey stuff.

That thing about books and their covers. Maybe he wasn't what she'd concocted in her mind for him to be.

Then again... maybe he was. And maybe she wasn't going to just believe everything Leah said about her son.

Age-old despair settled in her gut over her situation.

One day she wished to feel something else. Something good.

She'd forgotten what feeling good felt like.

Lathering up her hair, she breathed in the

spicy scent to distract herself from the burning sensation on her scalp. She'd gotten her hair caught on one of the beds before she left and had to pull it loose while hacking at it with a dull plastic knife. It had pulled more than it cut.

Pushing off from the wall, she rinsed her hair clean. Her legs shook from the effort to keep herself upright, and when she was done, she pawed at the handle to turn the faucet off.

Looking up, she found Leah through the open shower door, holding a large white towel. She stepped into it and the older lady helped her over to the stool before her legs gave out.

"I'll try to clean up your clothes, and bring you some of mine for in the meantime. But right now, you sit there and rest. I'm going to grab some of Thomas's."

Marlee watched as Leah slipped past the bathroom door. Murmuring could be heard, and then she was back, carrying a stack of clothes.

"Here you go."

She set them on the counter and turned her

back once more, allowing Marlee privacy.

Patting at her tender skin, she dried off the best she could, taking her time. Better slow than to end up face planting on the bathroom floor.

When she was mostly dry, she reached for the pile Leah had brought. A black t-shirt the size of Alaska was on top. The fabric was buttery soft and for several breaths, she just rubbed the pads of her fingers across it. Tears wet her eyes, and she didn't know why. It was a t-shirt. But it was the softest thing she'd touched in a long time.

Clearing her throat, she eased it over her head. It was like sinking into a cloud. She reached for the gray sweat pants, shakily pushing her legs into them. Not as soft, but so much better than the rough jeans she'd inherited from one of the girls. She shuddered, remembering the years she'd had nothing to cover her legs. Anything was better than that... but these, were a step above the jeans.

Leah turned around just as she was maneuvering them up her waist.

"Okay, hun. I bet that feels better, yeah? Now

let's get you back into bed."

Marlee froze. "*His* bed?"

Leah pressed her lips together nodding.

Marlee shook her head. She could sleep on the floor. Being in Ratchet's bed was too dangerous. She wouldn't sleep with him in return for these clothes. No.

Soft things meant nothing if they led to brutality.

"I told you, he won't hurt you," Leah reminded her, and this time she sounded a little more confident. "Come on."

Leah propped her body under Marlee's shoulder and guided her to the door. As they shuffled along, she became more nervous. Being captive in this new place meant plenty of uncertainties. And it also meant she was completely alone. Without her girls to keep her company. To remind her she was human.

They pushed through into the room that was dimmer than the bathroom, and she steeled herself for anything...

And she didn't know what she expected, but it wasn't *this*. Ratchet, shirtless in his bed waiting for her like she'd been purchased maybe, yeah. But him standing next to the dresser, looking nervously at a tray full of food? She hadn't expected that.

He seemed to be inspecting the items when he noticed she was there. Looking up at her, his expression went oddly soft. It stole her breath. Scared her more than his icy gaze had when she woke. Just for a second before it snapped back to its typical snarl.

There, yeah. That, she could handle.

"Brought you food." His gruff voice was low and he pulled back his shoulders, looking proud.

But it took several breaths for his words to register.

"For me?"

Why would he?

He stepped back, jamming his hands in his back pockets and stared at the food instead of her.

"You can have it all," he declared. "And if you

want more, I can bring you more. It's just right down the hall in the lounge."

Still leaning on Leah, Marlee examined the tray. There was so much. More than she'd seen in a year probably. The scent of tomatoes and garlic filled the room. And she spotted chocolate cake.

Her stomach rumbled in response. So long since she'd eaten anything like this. Just looking at the food gave her strength. She wanted to run to it, shove it down her throat as fast as she could. The desire was so strong a small whimper escaped.

She cleared her throat to cover it.

"H-how much?"

Ratchet frowned, and she clarified.

"What will it cost me?"

His confused gaze went to his mother, his mouth opening and closing with no answer.

"It's a gift," Leah answered for him. "He won't take anything from you for eating it."

Ratchet's scowl deepened until he seemed furious. His anger should have scared Marlee.

Angry people were hard to read. Would he blow up? Hit her? Do worse? But something about his reaction seemed... comforting.

How strange.

"It's yours," he snapped, flinging his arm in an arc over the dresser. "I want you to eat."

Marlee frowned. He was just giving her all this food. Why would he do that?

"Bed first," Leah interjected, leading Marlee over to it.

She pulled back the covers and eased herself down. The bed was soft, the sheets cool, and the thick down comforter so cozy she could cry. She'd been too scared when she woke to notice. Now it was like sinking into a piece of heaven.

If only she wasn't trapped here. Then maybe she could enjoy it.

"All right," Leah said, tossing Marlee a look full of warning. It said *be good*, and sent a chill down her spine. "I'll leave you to eat."

Marlee shook her head, but Leah ignored her. No. She couldn't leave her alone with the strangely angry man.

But the woman turned to Ratchet—who suddenly seemed bewildered—and murmured, "Call me if you need anything."

He opened his mouth, but again, nothing came out. And then Leah disappeared behind the door, the sound of it clicking behind her hitting Marlee just as hard as the lock had earlier.

Seven

Ratchet stared at the bedroom door as it clicked shut, wondering why his mother was in a hurry to leave. The female didn't look fixed yet. She didn't look whole, though she looked a hell of a lot better after the shower. And in his clothes.

Like she belonged in them.

Damn that got him fired up, didn't it?

The thought of a woman in his clothes had never done a thing for him before. In fact, he preferred to keep them far away from his things. The farther the better. But Marlee was different.

Seeing her when she emerged from the bathroom, wearing his t-shirt that could almost reach her knees...

He breathed through the emotions battering his chest at the memory. Fucking feelings he had no name or reference for.

Turning, he found her watching him from the bed.

Oh, she looked good like that too. In his bed like she was his.

Was this how it always started? The mating. Was this how his former brothers, Gash and Malcom, found their way? A feeling in your gut that both hurt and calmed in a single breath. One look at the right female and your entire world view changed, morphing into something that no longer revolved around you. It made her the sun and you the goddamn universe orbiting her. Was this... was she... the one who was supposed to burn away his past?

Yes. Her.

If what the voice told him was true... if he

could trust it...

Then he had to try hard for her. Not just because his insides were telling him to, but because if she could save *him*... there was hope for them all. His clan, his mother, their future.

Ratchet picked up the tray and carried it to the bed. Marlee tensed the closer he neared. But she would have to get used to him.

"You like pepperoni?" He kept his voice low. "Or would you rather have dessert first? I'd go for the cake if it were me. My mom's recipe. All the guys love it."

She looked away from the food to the black screen of the TV. "No thank you."

"Cookies then? If you start with something sweet first, your stomach won't reject it."

It was a trick he learned from his training. They were made to go hungry when the fathers thought they were too weak. The longer they made it without shifting, the stronger they were said to be. Ratchet had made it four days when he was only ten. Gash topped it the next time by half a day. Then Felix went one hour shy of five days before his cat emerged to save him.

But eating again after so long without was the worst part. Too long without makes the stomach see food as foreign.

Marlee stared at him, skeptical. "How would you know?"

"Just do."

Her eyes narrowed, taking him in, before she repeated, "No thank you."

She stared at the TV again. Maybe she wanted to watch it. But eating was most important right now.

"You have a favorite show?"

Seconds ticked by before she answered. "Used to."

"What is it?"

"Gilmore Girls."

Ratchet scowled. "Never heard of it."

"Not surprised," she muttered.

He set the tray on the foot of the bed and reached for the remote. Clicking the screen on, he pulled up Netflix and searched for the show.

"What is that?" Marlee asked, pulling his attention back to her.

"Streaming. It's the best way to watch TV."

Her eyes were big and confused. "I remember Netflix. They send DVDs in the mail. Like a delivery movie rental."

Shit. She'd missed the entire digital revolution.

"They don't do it like that anymore," he grumbled. "They send it straight to your TV now."

Her brow scrunched as she frowned. It was cute.

Shit. Cute?

The hell was wrong with him?

"How do they send it?"

"It's connected to the internet. Like email. It sends the data—"

Her gaze snapped to him and she looked like she wanted to roll her eyes. "I know what email is. But... how does this work?"

Ratchet moved closer to the bed. "You just

search for a show or movie or whatever. And then hit that button to start it."

"And it just… plays?"

"Yeah."

He pulled up the information for the most recent season of her show, *Gilmore Girls: A Year in the Life*, and hit start.

"Wait, what is this?" Marlee murmured. "A new one? I watched the series finale back before… before I was…" Her words stalled out as she watched the intro and then the first scene pull up. "Wow. Rory is all grown up."

That last part was tinged sad, and he realized that the woman on the screen would be about Marlee's age. It must remind her she'd lost time. He tried to imagine how that would feel, but he didn't know. He'd lost a lot, but he hadn't been tucked away somewhere while time marched on.

He paused the show and Marlee's gaze snapped to him.

"Wha… why'd you do that?"

"It makes you sad."

"So?"

"So, I'm not letting you watch it if it makes you sad."

She tilted her head, looking more confused than ever. "What if I want to be sad. Ever think of that? What if I choose it?"

Ratchet scowled at the female. "You want to be sad?" He'd never heard of such a thing. Who the hell ever *wanted* to be sad? It was just something you endured, not something you chose.

"I want to watch this show."

Even if it made her sad.

Well. Fine.

But only after he got what he wanted.

"I'll turn it on if you eat."

Marlee stared at him, her mouth hanging open. The split corner of her lip drew his attention. He wanted to reach over and feel it. Test it. See if it hurt. And if it did, find some way to make if feel better.

"You're bribing me to eat with Gilmore Girls?" Her question came out like a breath. Like she was speaking the unfathomable.

Ratchet straightened his shoulders. Bribing. Yeah, if he had to do something underhanded like that to get food in her belly, he would. Whatever was needed to see to her. He wasn't a good man. She should expect him to do bad things. Even if it was for a good reason.

"Yeah. I am." He picked up the tray and forked a piece of the chocolate cake. "The sweet stuff first. You'll feel better. You'll see."

Slowly, because she still looked frightened by his nearness, he brought the fork to her lips. But she didn't move to eat.

"Open," he demanded.

"If I eat that, I owe you. I don't want to owe you."

Owe him? It was true. She would owe him. But that didn't mean she shouldn't eat.

"You already owe me."

She frowned until a little crease formed between her dark brows. "How could I owe you?"

"For saving you earlier, in the shed. From my

leader, Felix. He would have hurt you. But I'm keeping you safe. I won't let anyone hurt you."

"Keeping me captive you mean."

He dipped his chin. "As long as it keeps you safe."

She stared into his eyes, digging for something, searching him out.

"Safe. Even from you?"

Her question was like a punch in the gut. It was simple enough, and an obvious one, since to her, they were hardly more than strangers. The problem was he didn't know the answer.

From the moment he found her asleep in the shed, he knew he needed to protect her. But how could a lion protect a lamb when he provided the most danger?

The voice inside, the beast that was emerging, so similar to his werecat yet so different, whispered. *Your heart will show you how.*

"Yes." He answered his female with confidence because inside he could feel the truth. "I will always keep you safe. Especially from myself."

Her eyes grew wide with surprise before narrowing again in distrust. "You could be lying."

She was smart, his woman. But he would prove himself.

"I could," he agreed. "But if you want to watch Gillicuddy Girls, you'll eat."

"Gilmore."

"That's what I said."

She blinked several breaths away. And then reached unsteadily for the fork. "I can feed myself."

"You're shaking. I will do it for you." He nudged the bite closer to her lips, urging her to comply. The chocolate was so close, it must be torturing her senses.

With a defeated sigh, she parted her lips and he pushed the fork in so carefully. Like he was feeding a cub. Careful with his female.

Her mouth closed around the bite and her eyes did too as he slid the fork back. She was savoring it. A moan of satisfaction eased from her throat and it hit Ratchet right in the crotch, springing his dick to life.

Aw, shit.

He couldn't deal with that fucker right now. He hadn't been attracted to a female enough to make him hard in months, and now wasn't the time for that.

Who was he kidding. With her, there would never be a time.

She might be his, and his heart might need her. But he could never show her his sick way of fucking. It was quick and hard and brutal. And there were plenty of women in the world who liked that. But Marlee... instinctually he knew, wouldn't.

She would want soft. Sweet. Gentle.

She would want careful touches and slow orgasms that lasted all night. Luxurious kisses that curled her stomach into knots, robbed her breath, and left her body numb with pleasure.

He could offer hard pounding that mixed pain and pleasure and left her a sweaty soaked mess on the floor.

He swallowed hard, willing his erection down just in time for her eyes to open.

"You like it?" he croaked out.

But her eyes were glazed with desire as she stared at the tray. "More. Please."

He fed her three more bites and every damn time, that moan of satisfaction. It was like food for his soul. Such a little thing maybe, using food to make her happy for a small piece of time, but it felt massive inside, where he was so broken.

"Milk?" she asked weakly.

"We only had one carton and it was opened. Not good for you."

She eyed him, using her middle finger to wipe a crumb from the corner of her mouth.

"I have more water. Or unopened OJ."

"Water would be nice."

He set the tray beside her on the bed and went to the fridge for another bottle. When he returned, she'd picked up the fork, helping herself to the rest of the cake.

"Slow down, little lamb," he murmured, twisting the cap off the water and handing it to her.

But he didn't think she heard him.

She gulped the water, spilling some of it down her cheeks, and shoved more cake between her lips.

Ratchet reached for the remote, pressing play on her show, and then pulled over a chair to sit beside her so he could watch her eat. In those moments, he felt more whole than he had in all his years. More satisfaction than any night with a warm willing body. More good than bad. More human than animal. And it had nothing to do with his dual nature. It was his heart, changing.

And it was because of *her*.

Eight

The credits rolled for the end of the show Marlee loved. Streaming. Netflix. It was nothing like the tiny boxy television she'd watched for years in the basement. It got only local channels and they were grainy. Ratchet's TV was crisp and so bright it almost hurt her eyes. She'd think it was some special television only rich people could afford. But looking around his room told her he wasn't wealthy.

Everything was simple. Clean, but well used. From the rug to the chipped dresser to the plain cotton bedsheets.

Which meant this was just a normal television and the thing she'd been watching for years was probably old as dirt.

She searched the darkness for Ratchet. After she'd eaten what she could, he shut off everything, leaving only the TV for light. Now she found him asleep in the chair he'd pulled over. It was between the bed and the wall. Too close to the door for her to escape.

But something else kept her inside the room now.

The fear of what waited for her beyond the door.

Leah said there was danger. Something worse than her son, who... didn't seem all that dangerous. Sure, Marlee could feel the restraint he operated under. She could feel that he *was* dangerous. Had maybe even done bad things. He just didn't seem dangerous *for her*.

He let her watch whatever she wanted. Fed her. Gave her clothes. Didn't ask to use her body.

And kept her a secret from the ones she'd seen in the lounge. From his leader, who was apparently Satan incarnate from the way they talked.

But he doesn't know who you belong to.

Everything would change when Ratchet found out. It would have to. He'd give her up. Unless Leah could get her out before then.

Marlee pushed down the panic that came with that thought, and focused on the sleeping man nearby.

He'd slouched in the seat so that his head could rest on the back. His blond hair was tousled, a few strands of it hanging over his closed eyes. His face was pointed in her direction. Like he'd fallen asleep watching her.

He'd taken the chair and given her his bed.

It was so unexpected. A captor giving instead of taking. It confused her inside. Made her feel safer when she should feel trapped.

The screen of the TV dimmed, preparing to shut off. It sent fresh panic to her middle.

Leaning over the edge of the bed, she

carefully eased the remote out of Ratchet's loose grip. She held her breath, only making a millimeter's progress at a time so she wouldn't wake him. But she was still shaking from the residual drugs in her system. Sleep would help. But she couldn't sleep in the dark.

She nearly had the remote free when her hand accidentally brushed against his.

He growled out a snarl, his eyes snapping open. Their blue nearly glowed in the darkness as he glared at her, and his fingers wrapped around her wrist like a vice, squeezing tight. He moved like lightning, striking so fast she couldn't have done a thing to prevent it.

"Ow!" she cried.

The remote clattered to the floor and Ratchet's angry face went slack with awareness. His gaze shot to her arm where he held it, and with the next blink, he dropped her like she'd scalded him.

Marlee scrambled backward until her back hit the headboard.

"Sorry." His voice whipped from his throat, rough and heavy with sleep. "I didn't mean to touch you."

She rubbed at her wrist. It didn't hurt as much as it had shocked. His touch was hot enough to burn her.

"Not used to having anyone near while I sleep. I don't..." He cleared his throat, sitting forward and running his palms roughly over his face. "I don't rest when other people are around."

Marlee huffed out a breath, forcing the panic down. "Why don't you?"

He stared at her through the dimness. The light from the TV reflected off his lips that were parted with heavy breathing.

"Never a good idea to be vulnerable."

Marlee swallowed hard. She'd lived that way too, for ten years. But before, when around the people she loved, she hadn't thought like that. So why here, in his home, did Ratchet need to be so vigilant?

"Your family would hurt you?"

"Not permanently. But yes. If it got them ahead somehow."

"What kind of family is that?"

"A fucked up one." He stood and went to the fridge, pulling out another bottle of water and a beer. "You get enough to drink?"

Marlee nodded, still rubbing at her wrist.

"Did I hurt you?" His question was low and soft. Tentative, like he didn't want to ask and was afraid of the answer.

"Not really."

He passed her the water and collapsed back into his chair, expression troubled. His knees spread wide, like he was trying to get comfortable and he dug into his pocket coming out with a ring of keys. Attached was a bottle cap opener in the shape of an animal's paw. He used it on the beer, flicking the lid into the nearby trashcan before taking a swig.

"I was just trying to get the remote."

He raised an eyebrow that morphed into a frown. He found the controller on the floor and set it on the comforter next to her legs and raised his bottle to his lips again.

"Was just gonna restart the show. I don't like sleeping in the dark." Oh, she shouldn't have told him that. What was she thinking?

Slowly, he pulled the bottle from his lips, staring at her like she'd given him her darkest secret to guard.

"You shouldn't tell me things like that," he said darkly. "Shouldn't tell anyone your weaknesses."

"I know." She did. It had slipped out.

"It's fine. I'll keep it tight," he vowed. "But around here, if you encounter anyone else, don't show your tender spot. Understand? We... *they* feed off weakness."

She nodded, feeling stupid for letting it out. She knew better. One time she'd confided in the dolls how the radio helped her feel connected to the rest of the world. The next day her captor had smashed it and told her she could have another one when she started working for it.

What a bastard.

She eyed Ratchet. Something about him had practically pulled the confession from her. Her instincts wanted to trust him when her mind warned her not to. Her instincts had never been wrong. But now, what if she was too broken and it was leading her astray?

What if she couldn't even trust herself anymore?

"I work tomorrow," he said, his tone going remorseful. "I'll have to leave you for a while. You'll stay here. You can rest. Watch your show. Whatever. But don't leave the room. Never leave here without me."

It was a warning, not a threat. She knew that now.

"I won't."

His eyes searched hers for honesty.

"The men you live with aren't kind."

"None of us are," Ratchet agreed.

"Us? Why do you say *us*? You've been kind. So far."

He shook his head, staring away at nothing. "Because it's you. I think if it was any other female, I'd be just as bad as them." Even though his words were strained, she could hear the regret in them, heavy and hopeless.

"What's different about me?"

He gazed at her, his eyes flickering with some unexplained emotion.

"I don't understand," she whispered.

Ratchet leaned forward, grabbing the remote and punching the button to restart the show. As the intro music played, he walked to the bathroom, turning the light on in there and then the lamp next to the bed.

"Sleep, lamb." The rumble of his voice sent a shiver rolling up her spine. But it didn't scare her. It soothed her. "I'll keep the lights on."

Marlee settled in, pulling the covers up to her chin.

If she was in danger tonight, it just didn't matter. Because she was clean, her belly was full, the bed was warm, and the lights were on.

Maybe she was still dreaming after all.

Nine

Ratchet held the marble between his thumb and forefinger, staring hard at it. It was perfect. A throwaway like everything else he found, but he saw value in it. The thing was emerald green and faceted inside like a jewel. Or... just like Marlee's eyes. He'd used his shirt to polish it to a shine.

Skittles cleared his throat from the driver's seat as the truck rumbled down a narrow alley way on the industrial side of Memphis. Ratchet was anxious to finish work. They only had two more stops to make before they called it a day.

The construction bin on the new wing of the casino needed dumping, and some barrels behind one of Bastian The Bastard's warehouses.

Then he could bring Marlee the gift he'd found her.

Leaving her this morning hadn't been easy even with his mom promising to keep an eye on her. She was fast asleep, and he'd stayed awake most of the night just watching her, catching a few Zs here and there. She'd had nightmares again, if her whimpers were anything to go by. And so many times, he'd reached for her, wanting to hold her so she'd know she was safe. But he'd made a promise to keep his hands to himself. And he did.

When she's ready you'll know.

The voice inside him was growing stronger, his instincts returning little by little. And it didn't resemble his sick animal at all. Every minute since finding Marlee, he grew stronger. Less sick inside. It was too early to say if he was healing or not. Maybe he'd just felt bad for so long anything better seemed like a miracle.

"You feel different today," Skittles said, his words barely louder than the radio that was screaming Papa Roach from the speakers.

Ratchet shot him a scowl. "Different how?"

Skittles turned down a new alley and brought the truck to a stop, clicking the radio off. At the back, Monster jump down from the ladder and started dumping the barrels in the bin.

"Better," Skittles murmured, watching in the rearview mirror. "Less sick. Is there something you need to tell me?"

Ratchet tucked the marble in his pocket and stared out the window. "Nope."

"If you've found a way to heal, I need to know."

"Just having a less shitty day I guess. Happens sometimes."

"Bullshit. There are no good days and you know it."

Ratchet reached for the door handle. He needed to help Monster.

"You need to think of the clan. We're getting

worse. No end to this in sight. You know how long I've been looking for a way. If something doesn't happen soon, Felix will be dead. Either because his human part can't cope or because one of our enemies has killed him."

Ratchet snapped his gaze around. "You say that like it's a bad thing. Maybe he needs to die."

Skittles' eyes narrowed to slits.

"You know what he's done. The lives he's ruined. He's no better than the fathers."

"None of us are," Skittles snapped. "Just because we haven't bred females yet, doesn't mean we aren't monsters."

Ratchet thought of the female in his bed. Was that where they were headed? Was he going to breed her and ruin her life like so many others had done. Was that what his instinct was telling him to do?

No. Never harm her.

No. The thing inside wouldn't let him. He could trust it. It wasn't dark like his cat had been. It was bright. If he could see it, he knew it would be blinding. And last night as he'd watched Marlee sleep, it grew so strong in his chest it burned. Hot inside him, like nothing he'd ever felt.

Somehow, he knew the thing would incinerate him if he stepped in the wrong direction.

The healing beast... the new beast... it would protect Marlee. From him. From anyone.

Which confirmed what Ratchet had been thinking over as the night hours stretched on.

Marlee was his mate.

He was hers.

Except... not *him*. The thing inside him.

Ours, it whispered. *She is ours.*

I can't have her, he thought back at it. *I'm shit. I don't deserve her.*

But she deserves you.

Ratchet went still inside at the beast's words. Not because he agreed, but because he could see what the thing meant. Marlee needed someone who could keep her safe from her past, safe from whoever might be after her. Someone who could provide a haven for her while she healed. Someone who would respect her boundaries and would take her *no* as law.

And by fuck… he was that person.

Seemed crazy as fucking hell, but it was true.

"All I'm saying is," Skittles continued. "If you know something, you owe it to your clan to share."

Ratchet glared at his brother. "I don't owe this clan shit. Neither do you. They already took it all out of our backs. I've already paid anything I owe in scars."

Skittles fumed, a denial on his lips, but Ratchet didn't let him make it.

"Malcom had it right, you know. And Gash. We called them traitors, but it was only because we didn't understand. There is someone out there who can fix us. When you find it, you'll see. It will rewrite everything you know. Rewrite your fucking DNA. Just like it did with them."

That's what was happening to him, wasn't it? The beast didn't feel familiar because it was new.

Whatever he'd been before wasn't just healing. It was transforming.

Skittles stared hard at him. "How. Do. You. Know?"

Ratchet let out a ruthless laugh and stared out the windshield.

"Did you find yours?" Skittles whispered the question like saying it out loud would send him straight to hell.

Ratchet set his jaw so tight he thought it could crack.

Skittles dug in the pocket of his flannel shirt, producing the photo he'd shown him in the lounge and shoving it toward him. "Is she one of these?"

"Even if I did, even if she was... why *the fuck* would I ever tell you?"

"Goddamn it," Skittles growled, pressing the photo inches from Ratchet's nose. "Look at this picture and tell me if one of them is yours."

Ratchet didn't look at the photo. He stared at his brother. The way his eyes were bugged out and desperate. The way the vein at his temple flicked. The way his skin flushed, muting color in his tattoos.

"Why would I trust you that much?"

"Because one of them is mine," Skittles snarled, "and I have to find her. I have to find her *now*, before something horrible happens to her."

Shiiiiiiit.

Ratchet's chest went numb.

He snatched the picture from Skittles' grip, staring at it hard.

"Which one?"

"I'd never fucking give that away."

Ratchet smirked to cover up all the *oh shit* raging inside him. "Smart. Felix know?"

"No one knows. And no one better find out. I will take what's left of your skin if you tell a soul."

He let the threat roll off his back. Skittles, the bastard, had just given him his biggest vulnerability. If Ratchet wanted, he could have him by the short hairs.

But he didn't want that.

Which was new. Not wanting to have power over his brother.

"How do you know something hasn't already happened to her?"

"I don't," Skittles rasped. "So if you know something, Ratchet, you'd better fucking tell me now."

Shit. He couldn't reveal his mate. It was too dangerous. Even if Skittles was in the same desperate position. Ratchet couldn't risk *anyone* knowing about Marlee. But especially the Alley Cat second in command. What if the cat was lying?

"I can't help you—"

The passenger door to the cab swung open and Monster's snarling scarred up face took up the opening.

"You gonna get out here and help me dump this shit or what, asshole?"

Ratchet couldn't make his mouth work.

Monster's eyes dropped to the photo. Frowning, he ripped it from Ratchet's grasp and brought it right up to his face. "What's this?"

"Ratchet was just about to tell me where that picture came from," Skittles shot off.

"I fucking told you. I don't know." It wasn't a lie.

"I can read you, shithead. I know you're hiding something."

"Just because you found a female that catches your eye doesn't mean—"

A burst of fury filled the cab and Skittles' eyes seemed to glow. It was so familiar, the way his animal used to look but different.

And Ratchet reacted, the burning beast inside him rearing up as if to fight. As if he could even pull it forth from his body.

Skittles must have come to the same conclusion because nothing else happened. They just snarled, chest rumbling with unsatisfied growls.

"I..." Monster's voice sounded hollow. Empty. And it brought the attention back to him. "I know where this is."

Ratchet swung his gaze around to the scarred

up brother. He looked like he'd taken a hit. Like the fucking devil had his heart in his fist. He shook, the hand holding the picture rattling like a leaf in the wind.

Monster cursed, backing away from the truck door. He walked five steps and turned, like he couldn't decide what his body was supposed to do. Skittles was out of the cab and around the other side before Ratchet had jumped from the passenger seat.

"I know... I know... fuck, this is..."

But before either of them could ask what he meant, his hand—the one holding the photo—burst into flames.

Monster dropped the flimsy piece of paper and Ratchet watched in horror as it fluttered to the ground, the corner of it already on fire.

"*Fuck.*" Skittles ran forward, stomping it out as if it was his actual woman and not just a picture of her.

"Shit!" Monster's eyes peeled wide, all the whites showing, as he stared at his burning hand like it was foreign.

"What the hell?" Ratchet eased forward. The brother was acting like the fire didn't hurt. "Monster?"

Frowning hard, Monster turned his hand palm up. The flame followed him, engulfing his entire hand. Still, he just watched it, seeming as confused as Ratchet felt. He squeezed his fingers into a fist, turning the fire into a ball. It didn't consume him. No blistering. No burning. And it didn't spread.

"It's like..." Ratchet couldn't make the words come.

"Malcom," Skittles finished.

When the clan hunted him down to make him pay for being a traitor, he'd mated and healed. Fully shifter. But his animal was nothing like the cougar he'd been when he was one of the Alley Cats. He was changed. His animal was made of fire. The body of a lion with a mane of flames. Could spit it from his mouth, and never burn.

The way Monster's hand didn't burn.

"You fucking piece of shit," Skittles spat. "You've been hiding this, haven't you? You have your animal back, like Malcom, and you never said a thing. While the rest of us rot away, you said nothing."

Ratchet couldn't blame Monster for making that choice. He was making it himself. Marlee was changing him, and he was hiding it. Damn right, he was. Until he was strong enough to protect her from the others.

Shit, the only time an Alley Cat looked out for the whole was when it benefitted him. Brotherhood was only on paper, not in the heart. And loyalty was to power not the powerless.

Monster's glare snapped to Skittles. "I would *never*," he growled. "Your fucking picture did this. Not me. Brought fire to my hand."

"Bullshit."

Monster fumed. "You'll be taking that accusation back, candy ass. Or I'll be taking it out of your back."

And Monster would have the right. You

couldn't just falsely accuse your brother of treason without consequences.

But Monster's words seemed to make the flame fade. The brutality in his eyes, the revenge on his heaving breath as he glared at Skittles... within seconds, the fire was gone as if had never been. As if they'd all imagined it. No soot. No smoke.

The only evidence that it had happened at all was the charred corner of the picture Skittles gripped between his fingers.

"How did you do it?" Skittles demanded. "How did you call fire out? Can you shift?"

"No. There's no animal inside. It's fucking dead. Just like yours. Just like everyone's."

Ratchet stared between them. Because his wasn't. There was something inside him. Something called forward by Marlee. He couldn't know what it was or if it would ever amount to what Malcom had, but he wasn't letting it fade away.

"The... the picture," Monster huffed. "The

female in the picture. *She* did this."

Skittles frowned. "How?"

"She... I... they..."

"Which girl?" Skittles stomped forward, shoving the photo in Monster's face.

The breath seemed to stall in Monster's chest as he stared at the photo again. Ratchet stared at it too.

"*Her*," Monster breathed, pointing one shaking finger to a woman with ratted blond hair.

And the way he said it caught Ratchet around the throat. *Her.* How many times had the voice whispered that word to him when he looked at Marlee. Her, her, her.

Skittles' shoulders eased and he stared hard at Monster. "She yours?"

Monster shook his head, opening his mouth to answer, but nothing came out. He narrowed his eyes at the girl in the photo.

"Say it," Skittles demanded, but his voice had lost any threat. It sounded all off. Almost... scared, but Ratchet knew better.

Unless this was really happening. He remembered the fear he felt when he found Marlee in the shed.

"Yes," Monster gritted. "*Fuck*. Yes. She's mine. And I know where she is."

Shit.

"Where?" Skittles crowded Monster. The two of them were a fucking spark away from brawling.

Monster pressed his lips together, refusing.

"You have to tell me."

"Why? So you can use her against me?" Monster roared. "Whatever the fuck she just did to me, was none of my doing. Now I can't even say out loud that she's nothing. Whatever is moving inside won't let me. And you want me to tell you what I know? Here's what I know. She's a vulnerability. And Alley Cats can't have vulnerabilities."

"What if she's not?" Ratchet blurted.

Both brothers turned their shrewd gazes on him, and the voice inside growled in warning.

Careful.

"What if she's not a vulnerability? What if she makes you stronger?"

"How could she?" Monster asked, but Ratchet could see the wheels turning in Skittles' mind. He'd already been thinking along the same lines.

"You couldn't hold a ball of fire before seeing her. I'd say that's progress. What if it's like with Malcom, and she can heal you?"

Monster's mouth did a shrug, twisting his scarred chin. "Even more of a reason to keep her secret. Felix would never let one of us become more powerful than him."

True, but it was already happening. How could Felix ever stop it? Whatever power he held over the clan now was just leftover fear from before.

Ratchet shrugged. "So... what? You know how to find your female. The Sorcera said the only way to break the spell is to have a change of heart. To learn to love. What will you do, Monster?"

He straightened his shoulders, jutting his chin out stubbornly. "Nothing. I'm broken. No female is going to change that."

"Well, fuck you," Skittles snapped. "I promised the clan I would find a way to heal us. And I'm going to try." He poked his finger at a dark-skinned female with big eyes. "This one's mine. Tell me how to find her."

Monster's whole demeanor changed as he looked from the picture to Skittles and back.

"What kind of game are you playing?"

"No game," Skittles ground out. "*Her.* Something inside whispered it when you saw yours, right? Tell me I'm wrong."

Monster already gave that away without even trying, but he kept quiet. Ratchet held his breath. Had all three of them really found the answer to their curse? He didn't believe in coincidences. If it was true... this was fate.

"You're going fucking apeshit inside because you don't know if she's all right. You want to sniff her out like the cats of old would have done. Find her and put her under your protection even though you don't have an animal to make you strong."

Monster's chest chugged for breath.

"Two seconds. That's all it took." Skittles low voice rattled the air. "Two blinks. Two heartbeats, and you were altered enough you'd die for her. And you don't even fucking *know her.*"

Ratchet could feel his eyes were huge. His throat was like a cactus swallowing cotton.

"How do you know that?" Monster hissed.

"Because," Skittles growled. "I'm living it. Somehow, some way... we are in the same fucking boat, brother. Now what are we going to do about it?"

A million emotions flashed over Monster's face. Hope and determination, defeat and fury. Suspicion, cycling back to hope, cycling back to defeat until his expression melted back into nothing.

"Nothing," he said, reiterating what his face spoke. "We do nothing."

"How can you say that?"

"Because. We are powerless."

Skittles shook his head, opening his mouth to argue but Monster stopped him.

"Take a closer look at that picture."

"The hell are you talking about? I've been staring at it for two days now."

"Look. Closer."

Ratchet peered over his shoulder trying to see whatever Monster was talking about. He blurred out the girls and focused on other pieces of the setting. And when he saw it, there in the foreground, just a hint of an object he'd seen a thousand times before... his entire world started spinning.

"There," he rumbled, pointing to the edge of the photo, near where Monster had burned it.

The faint glow of a silver skull too close to the camera. It was the top of a walking cane. The kind you imagined a pimp might own just for show, or to beat his girls with. But the owner of this one was no pimp. He was practically a fucking god. The Lord of Memphis.

Bastian Marx.

Bastian the Bastard as Ratchet liked to think of him.

Human through and through, but cunning enough to have all the shifters in Memphis pressed tight under his thumb. He owned half of the city and every one of the casinos. He ran drugs, guns, whatever could make him a buck. And he used everybody he came in contact with. Both the Junkyard Dogs pack and the Alley Cats had done his dirty work for years.

They learned early on not to ask questions. The cats disposed of his trash... no matter what was in it. The dogs worked deep security, guarding Bastian's most important players.

Skittles squinted at the skull, shaking his head. "No way. That can't be what I think it is."

But he couldn't deny it. Not really. Bastian's skull had a specific detail that the one in the photo mirrored. The left eye—just like his own in real life—was blacked out with a patch.

"Shit," Skittles spat. "Fuck. Bastian has our females."

Ratchet struggled for air. *Bastian* had hurt Marlee. He'd starved her. Drugged her. Made her scared. Took her from her family and kept her locked away for ten fucking years.

Anger coursed through his veins, diluting his blood. He wanted revenge. Wanted to rip the human to pieces and scatter him over the Mississippi River for what he'd done.

And the worst part? The *fucking worst* part?

He worked for the man. Had helped make all his shitty deeds possible. He'd contributed to Bastian's empire. Like all the cats. Turned a blind eye for a little money. Or just because he could.

But if he'd known... if Ratchet had known the man was kidnapping and holding females, he would've...

No.

He would've done shit to stop him. That was the fucking truth of it.

Felix had held women at the warehouse plenty of times and Ratchet had never lifted a claw to stop it. The fathers before them had done even worse, and no one blinked. The Alley Cats didn't stand up for the hurting. They didn't do what was right. They took advantage. They harmed. And nothing would have changed that.

Except a curse, the voice inside whispered. *You're changing. Already changed. They will too*.

For the first time ever, Ratchet didn't begrudge what the witches did to them. Instead, he realized it was necessary. The cats had been a threat to their people, the Ouachita clan. But worse than that, they'd threated their brother's mate. Threatened Gash's pregnant female. The Sorcera had done what it took to protect her.

Ratchet wished to god they had some fucking Sorcera of their own right about now.

Monster ran a hand through his hair. "Maybe we could talk to Malcom. See if he'll help us get them free. We show up with him, no one could tell us no."

Ratchet shook his head. "Malcom will eat you before you can even get the first word out. Remember what he said?"

"If we come around again, no warning," Skittles murmured. "He burns us to a crisp. And if we die, there would be no one to help our females. At least with us alive... there's a chance. It might take years before we find a way to get them." He stared up at Monster, fury rolling off him. "But we will get them."

Monster set his jaw so hard his teeth cracked. His fists clenched. His eyes blazed hot.

"In the meantime, we work for the bastard, knowing he has what's ours? You telling Felix? We doing this as a clan?"

Skittles stepped close to Monster, staring into his churning gaze. "We tell *no one*. We watch. We wait. And when the time comes... we fucking pounce."

Ratchet planned to be around when the moment came. Because he was getting revenge for his woman, for the things she'd endured. He had a lot of making up to do for his part, for knowing Bastian was evil and never doing a thing to stop him when he had the power to do so.

Start by loving her. Repair the damage done to her heart.

Ratchet didn't know how to love. Didn't know how to fix something as delicate as Marlee. But when he got home, he was going to try. He would dig into her, sweep away her fears, her suspicion. He was going to walk her through her own shadows and into his. If she could handle them… she'd make it through anything.

Ten

Marlee paced the floor of Ratchet's room, every step bringing her nerves closer to the edge. She was confined. Just like she'd always been. Stuck. The damn door wasn't locked, but she wasn't able to leave.

All the same.

She woke to the sun streaming in through his blinds. They'd been slitted halfway to let the light in, but keep the eyes out, and it was a nice change from waking in the dank dark basement. That little bit of access to the outside world had anchored her. Convinced her she was okay here in his room, by herself.

But now the sun had set and the light was gone.

Darkness was encroaching, reminding her of days on end in the basement without light. When her captor used her fear to persuade her.

All it did was cripple her.

The same as it was doing now.

And she couldn't turn the lamp on because it would draw suspicion to Ratchet's room. Which was supposed to be empty.

When Leah brought her lunch, she'd reminded her to keep quiet. Watch TV on low. Mind her steps because the offices were just below her on the main level of the warehouse.

But she'd needed to move when the sun sank so low she could barely discern the shadows. So she kept to the thick rug that covered the floor, hoping her footsteps were quiet enough.

The more minutes that ticked by, the darker the room became. Like every breath was dragging the sun further below the horizon. And those breaths were coming faster as her panic grew. She tried to slow them, but it only made it worse. Tears built in her lids as she chanted, "It's okay, it's okay. Don't forget, don't forget..."

You are Marlee Benson. You are twenty-eight years old. You were last free on your eighteenth—

The thump of heavy boots approached, stopping right outside the door, and Marlee slammed her mouth shut.

Seconds ticked off and her tears spilled over her lids, her heart thundering with adrenaline.

Fight or flight. Run. Scream.

The handle rattled, twisting slowly... and then the door eased open, streaming light in. The sudden change blinded her and instinctually, she cowered backward, hoping like hell this wasn't Felix. Or the ones she'd met in the lounge. Or Leah with more warnings about staying quiet and in the dark. Or anyone except Ratchet who could turn on the lights and make sure no one found her.

The door clicked shut and the boots came

closer. But her eyes hadn't adjusted, and the unknown had her fear soaring to nuclear levels. She pressed her lips together to hold in a whimper that was guaranteed to transform into a scream if she let it free.

The boots stopped in front of her and she blinked over and over, trying to make her eyes work.

"Marlee?"

The voice was Ratchet's. And the relief of hearing it was so crushing she moved without thinking.

She flung herself forward and he let out a soft *oof* as she connected with his chest. Her arms went around his waist in the blackness of the room. He smelled faintly of ash. More campfire than cigarettes. And the spicy scent of the shampoo she'd used. She pressed her face into his chest so she could cry without worrying who heard her.

And she let it all out.

What are you doing? Too close. Too close.

Her mind screamed at her to stop. To move away. But her body couldn't listen. In that single confusing moment, captor or not, he felt too… safe.

The sounds of her fear were muffled by his shirt as his big arms eased to circle around her. He moved so carefully. Like he was afraid of breaking her. Ratchet didn't know how to hug, but she didn't care. Because he felt good. Solid. A brick wall. An oak.

Steady.

One palm smoothed up her spine to gently grip her neck. She'd been grabbed by the neck before. Usually rough, reminding her she was owned by a bastard. But Ratchet's hand on her neck didn't scare her. There was no threat to it. It only said, *I'm here, I've got you.*

"What is it, lamb?" he ground out. "Tell me."

"It got dark," she whispered. She wasn't supposed to break down so easily. She'd been strong for so many years. Held her tears in when the others lost it, because she'd been there the longest and knew they were pointless. Now here, with nobody around to see but him, she couldn't do it anymore.

"Shit, woman. Don't cry," he croaked, regret coloring his voice dark.

As if she could make it stop. As if she had a choice. She *never* had a choice.

"You can't tell me that!" she cried into his thick chest. "It doesn't help."

"I wasn't supposed to be gone this long. We got hung up at one of the stops and then I wanted to get food to bring you. But Skittles got a call and we came on home. I'm… shit… I'm *sorry*."

The word sounded odd on his lips. Like he didn't ever say it. He didn't seem like the type of man who apologized for anything. But he was doing it for her.

She nodded against his chest, pushing back the terror. Gulping air to stem the tears. The deep breaths helped.

Lights. Turn on the lights.

She couldn't say it. All she could do was beg

silently.

"Won't happen again," he promised. "Shhh."

His thumb pressed into the side of her neck, smoothing up to the pressure point behind her ear while his other arm tightened a fraction to pull her in even closer.

"I know something," he said roughly. "It might help. You wanna hear it?"

She didn't answer, but he went ahead anyway.

"When I was a little cub and very afraid, I learned how to beat any fear. Back then, I was afraid of tight spaces. My father found out and he taught me a lesson."

His voice had gone harsh even though his hands on her were still gentle. She held on tighter.

"He said the only way to conquer a fear is to fear something bigger. He made sure I feared him more than anything else."

A chill rolled from her head to her toes. So Ratchet had a lousy father too. Was it a Memphis thing?

"That wasn't the way. But it taught me how. There's really only one way. And that's to face those fuckers and do battle with 'em."

She'd done a lot of facing the darkness. It hadn't helped. Ratchet was wrong.

"You have to make your courage greater than your fear. Until your fear feels little and you feel only... brave."

Her tears slowed, even though it was still dark. Ratchet's story had distracted her.

"I had to do it alone," he murmured. "But you don't have to. Face it here, with me. Open your eyes, lamb."

How did he know her eyes were shut?

"Can we just turn on the light?" she begged.

"Yes." His hot breath hit her ear. "We can. But you won't feel any stronger. Open your eyes."

She didn't want to do it, but he was right. If he turned the lights on now, she'd feel like a failure. This little breakdown will have meant nothing.

His hand moved to her chin, tilting her face up. With a shuddering breath, she forced her lids open. She saw nothing but shadows. Exactly as she expected. And again, that familiar panic climbed her spine.

But Ratchet's growling voice anchored her. Kept her from spinning into an anxiety tornado.

"Your name is Marlee *Fucking* Benson. You are twenty-eight years old. You had a dog named Jem," he began. "You were last free on... it doesn't matter. You'll be free again."

She let out a sob of a different kind. She had to believe it or she had nothing to live for. If the darkness was all she had, then she had nothing.

"Someone has found you," he rasped. "And he cares. Don't forget. Don't forget. Don't forget."

Her eyes stayed open. And maybe it didn't count because she didn't feel brave at all. She felt like this man was holding her up, making her strong when she didn't want to be.

But it didn't matter.

Because she *stood*. She stood in the dark. And her tears dried up. Her fear faded. It wasn't gone, it was just *less*. She'd battled it back, like he said she could.

Eventually, Ratchet pulled away, and she heard his boots thumping on the floor. It wasn't so easy keeping her eyes open with him not right there, but she was determined to do it.

Moments later, she heard the click of the lamp and the glow of the light blinded her. She blinked, letting her eyes adjust.

Ratchet was there when she could see again. He stood so close. Practically pressing into her. He reached forward as if to touch her face.

Too close, too close.

Marlee jerked away from his touch. Mostly out of habit. But in the light, being this close was difficult.

He let his hand fall and looked away to the door.

"Did you eat the breakfast I left you?"

She nodded. He'd left muffins and milk on the night stand. Something homemade. Probably his mom's because they were good, like the cake.

"And my mother brought you lunch?"

"Yes. She said I needed to turn off the TV if it got dark. So I did."

He eyed her silently.

"I have a surprise for you."

Marlee frowned, her stomach somersaulting. And not in a good way.

Her captor always had surprises for her and the other dolls. They were never good ones.

Surprise, no food tonight. Surprise, I'm turning the heat off. Surprise, I heard from your father... or rather about your father. He's dead. And you'll be mine forever, doll.

She hated surprises.

"A surprise?" Her mind raced with possibilities, none of them good.

Would Ratchet really turn this victory into something twisted? Was he like that? Her captor had been.

Ratchet nodded. "I need to wash work off first, and hunt us down some food. Then I'll show you. Okay? Give me an hour."

"Okay."

"I think you'll like it," he said, unsure.

And then he said things like that. Like he cared whether or not she liked what he was doing.

His lips pressed into a tight line and then he nodded, as if he was giving himself some internal pep talk.

She swallowed hard, trying to remember that Ratchet hadn't hurt her. Not at all. In fact, he'd only taken care of her. And had kept his promise not to touch her. Until she'd flung herself at him.

He pushed around her, strolling to the closet. She watched as he gripped the bottom of his shirt and swiftly pulled it over his head, tossing it on the floor. He missed the laundry basket by an inch, and she had the fleeting thought that he was like any normal man.

Or maybe not. Because his body wasn't simply normal.

His strong muscles rippled as he moved, capturing her attention. She'd never seen a man so perfectly built. Like he was sculpted from some artist's clay with care. Every ridge, perfected.

Every dimple carefully put in place.

But then she got a good look at his powerful back and gasped at what she saw there.

In his skin, was a roughly shaped S that stretched across his shoulder blades, slanted to his ribs, and curved around to end as waist. Small cuts of healed scar tissue formed the letter, though she couldn't guess what it meant.

Ratchet twisted, finding her horrified gaze, and frowned.

"What happened to you?" she whispered.

He looked away, pulling a fresh shirt from the dresser before he answered. "The scars, do they bother you?"

Again, worried about what she thought?

She could tell him yes. Maybe it would help him keep his distance.

But he seemed to be hanging on to her answer like it was keeping him from falling over some edge. And she'd never liked liars, so she wasn't going to be one now.

She shook her head, and he let out the breath

he'd been holding. "Do they bother you?"

He shrugged. "I used to be proud of them. They made me strong. Hard. But now…"

"Now what?"

He stared hard at her, his gaze going raw and stealing her breath for several beats.

"Now I wish I wasn't so hard."

Marlee nodded. She understood what he meant. She knew how it felt to wish you hadn't gone through hell. To wish you could have stayed the person you were before life broke you into pieces, and then shoved you roughly back together, making you something completely different. Something jagged and frayed. Something hard to handle, hard to love.

It made you hopeless.

But at least she wasn't alone.

Ratchet had gone through a hell of his own. And somehow, it helped knowing she wasn't the only broken one in the room.

Eleven

Ratchet stared down at his stubborn erection as the water from the shower crashed over his body.

He was going to win her. Marlee. He knew exactly what he had to do. And the way she'd run to him when he walked in the door had only confirmed it. Her body against his had felt like the missing piece of a puzzle. It was the plug that filled that empty hole in his chest he'd carried with him for his entire life.

That feeling of wholeness made him harder

than he'd ever been in his entire life. Aroused him deeper than any physical attraction.

He wanted closer to Marlee. Wanted more of that feeling. Wanted her to hold on to him all needy, like she did for those few precious minutes.

But he had to win her. Convince her he was the one. Convince his bedraggled animal that he could love someone. Her. Put another person's needs over his own.

But could he? Could he really?

Was his heart capable of it? Opening to another and doing all that intimate shit that bonded two people together?

He didn't know. But he knew he wanted it to be possible. With Marlee.

So... he needed to convince her, his animal, and *himself*.

Shit.

And all that when fucking nobody believed in him. Not even himself.

This is the way to heal. You, but also the clan.

You go first, the others will follow.

It was the only way to protect her how she needed. Ratchet had to be powerful to keep her safe from Bastian. From the clan. Healing his animal was the only way, and she was the only one who could do it.

But how the hell could he mate Marlee like he needed to? When she was so afraid of his touch. When she'd faced horrors he knew nothing about in Bastian's care. How could Ratchet ever make her feel safe enough to want him. And even if he could... he'd never be good enough for her like he was.

Too hard. Too rough. Too fucked up.

But he knew the answer to that one too, and his raging boner didn't appreciate it one fucking bit.

No sex.

The way to win Marlee was to find her heart and make a home there. Like she was starting to make in his. His lamb didn't need anyone owning her body. Not while she was a captive. Not with the fear so deep in her bones that it seeped out with every word.

Ratchet twisted the shower faucet to turn the water off. His dick was still hard from moments he'd spent holding Marlee, but he wasn't touching it. He'd spent too much time with his hand in the past, and he wasn't doing it now, with his girl so close by. The thing would just have to go away on its own.

Stepping out of the shower, he stared at his reflection in the fogged mirror.

Win his mate. That was the mission.

It would break the curse, which would make him strong enough to protect her. Strong enough to save the dolls, and start his clan on the road to recovery.

Monster and Skittles were ready to change. But right now, they were all as powerless as Marlee had been. As the other girls were.

All of them so fucking powerless.

Ratchet was going to bring it back. Restore them all, starting with himself and his sweet, scared mate.

He wrapped a towel around his waist and reached for the door, but then stopped, remembering the clothes he'd brought into the bathroom with him. He typically didn't give one shit about modesty. It was no big thing to shifters who changed forms often. But he could cover up for Marlee until she was used to him.

Doing a quick dry off, he jerked his jeans up his legs, not bothering to hook the button, and pulled a t-shirt over his head. There. He was covered.

Walking out into the room, he stopped short.

Marlee stood by the closet, the jeans he wore earlier hanging over her arm. She had his wallet in one hand and was staring into the palm of her other.

He cleared his throat and she looked up.

"I was cleaning up," she rushed out. "Putting the laundry in the basket, and this fell out."

She showed him what was in her palm, ruining one part of his surprise. The gift he'd found for her in the trash was cradled in her hand. And against her pale skin, it looked even closer to her eye color. It was perfect. But now he couldn't give it to her the way he'd planned.

"It's scratched a little. I'm sorry. I didn't mean to. Was it very important?"

"Kind of." He cleared his throat again, not liking the way his voice sounded. "But it's okay—" He was about to tell her it had come from the trash when she interrupted.

"Maybe I can fix it. I saw on the news one time that toothpaste can take scratches and scuffs out."

Well, fuck. Now she was trying to fix the broken thing he'd brought her. This attempt to court her wasn't starting out so well.

He reached forward, pecking it from her hand and jammed it in his pocket. Then he took his wallet, shut it in the dresser drawer, and tossed the jeans into the basket.

"I'll be right back," he said, escaping through the door before she could say anything else.

He took a deep breath and made his way to

the kitchen. Food and drinks. Then he'd show Marlee the rest of the surprise.

He bypassed the lounge. The party wasn't swinging yet, but he wanted something better than pizza and shit for tonight. If that meant he had to cook something up, then he would. And maybe Marlee wouldn't mind too bad if it was burnt.

But in the kitchen, he found his mom at the counter, quickly shoving food containers into a large paper bag. Her back was to him as she muttered, "I told you, Fang. The food is for Ratchet, and you can't have any. None, okay? He's finally eating, and he's going to want all of it. So buzz off. I'll make you some cookies later. Deal?"

"It's me."

Her head came around. "Oh, good. Here." She shoved the bag in his hands. "Take this. It's drawing too much attention."

"What is it, ma?"

She wiped her hands on a towel as her eyes shifted to the door and back to him. "Pasta. Salad.

Bread. Dessert."

"You didn't have to make us nothing."

"Yes, I did," she whispered. "She needs good food. Needs to get stronger, whether you like it or not."

Ratchet snapped his head back in surprise, and her eyes seemed to soften.

She thought he meant to hurt Marlee? Hadn't he kept his promise not to touch her? Hadn't he fed her and let her sleep in his bed and brought her a gift?

"Oh, son," she said regretfully, her shoulders slumping low. "I know what you're doing. You think you've found a mate, and you want to get her with child because it's what you're supposed to do. What you've been taught to do. But she doesn't need that, and this clan doesn't need any young, understand? Let her be. Let her heal. And then let her go."

Never.

The mere idea of letting Marlee go was a grip around his throat, threatening to choke him out.

"It's not like that."

She pressed her lips together, her worried gaze searching him.

"I've seen this so many times before, Thomas. I see the change in you."

He shook his head, staring away to avoid her guilt. It triggered the guilt that had been fading in him with every hour he spent with Marlee.

"She can heal me," he admitted, and looked back to catch his mom's expression. "She can break the curse. Give me my power back."

And that was when he saw it. Something he never saw in his mother. Something she'd obviously spent a lot of time concealing, masking. For what... survival?

Fear. He saw fear.

So blunt and stark. It wasn't much different than the fear he saw in Marlee. No, it was nearly the same.

His mother was afraid of him being healed? Of him regaining his power...

Ratchet narrowed his gaze.

She's a captive. Like mate.

The new beast whispered the truth to him, and he couldn't understand how he didn't see it before. His mother was a captive to the clan just like Marlee had been to Bastian. She was fed and cared for, and paid for the job she did. But a captive all the same. To their violence and the results of it. To the past and what the fathers put her through. To the future she'd lost sticking around to care for him and his brothers.

She was captive, and Ratchet was the one who'd kept her here.

Shit.

New guilt poured over him.

Why hadn't he seen it before?

You weren't ready. Your heart is growing stronger.

And instinct told him there would be more painful revelations to endure before he was completely healed. Before the curse could break and he could give Marlee and his mom back what too many people had taken from them.

He reached forward, wanting to touch her somewhere. A hug, hold her hand. It had been ages since he let her that close.

But it wasn't the right time. He wasn't fixed yet. And she wouldn't understand.

"You said you see changes," he reminded.

"Yes, but—"

"That's just the beginning. This clan is going to become something new. And it starts with me. I'm going to fix our wrongs."

He turned to leave, getting all the way to the kitchen door before she answered.

"Thomas."

Looking back over his shoulder, he met her sad gaze, and knew she didn't have faith in him. But he couldn't blame her. He'd just have to *show* her.

"Don't make promises you can't keep."

Twelve

It's just a marble. Just a tiny jewel-toned marble. He couldn't be that mad.

Marlee sat on the chair cross-legged, chewing her thumbnail to a nub while she waited for Ratchet to return.

She'd only wanted to pick up the room a little. It was starting to feel stuffy. And maybe look at Ratchet's driver's license to see how old he was. Or to find out *something* about the man who cared for her.

That's what she told herself.

But part of her was still looking for ways to escape. Any little crack in the armor that could help her get out faster. Because the other girls were still trapped until she got their picture to the FBI.

The picture she'd somehow lost.

"It's got to be in the shed," she murmured.

Which made getting free even more of a challenge, because she couldn't just run. She needed to find the photo. Then run.

Don't run.

The thought fluttered through her mind. It was always there, the desire to give in just to make things better, but she chased it off. Stockholm was a serious thing, and she'd fight it until her last breath.

Until she had true freedom again, she would never be done trying to escape.

Even if this was the safest she'd felt in a decade.

Even if Ratchet's strong arms had felt like a fortress around her.

Even if he made her want things she'd never had before. Stupid things. Like... friendship. Or more. True friendship that wasn't forced on her. She loved the other girls as much as she could. Even the ones who'd left her there to endure after they'd paid off their debts.

But she hadn't *chosen* any of them. And they hadn't chosen her.

Her heart raced as she remembered the way Ratchet had gripped her neck. Like he'd stand by her side through anything. She wanted devotion like that.

But then she'd screwed up his marble, so maybe that was enough to make him change his mind.

And... he was *holding* her here. So there was that too.

And her mind was too jumbled to think straight. She'd slept the drugs off, but there was still so much adrenaline and fear and worry in her system.

Breathe, Marlee.

The door eased open and Ratchet pushed through, carrying a giant paper bag.

Her surprise.

Her gut cramped in warning at the sight. Nothing good was ever carried in paper bags.

He set the bag on the dresser, not meeting her gaze. The snarl he wore as his go-to expression twisted his lips and furrowed his brow. He stalked to the closet, flicking through the hangers until he pulled a gray hoodie sweatshirt free. Then he finally looked at her, mouth open like he was about to say something, but stopped.

His shoulders dipped and he fisted the sweatshirt at his side. "What is it? What has you looking like that, Marlee?"

She liked that he used her name. Liked the way he said it. Careful, like he wanted to make sure every syllable was heard. She'd hated being called Thirteen. As if she was so insignificant she didn't deserve an identity.

"Like what?"

"Like I'm going to eat you. Like I haven't kept

you safe since the moment I found you. Like you didn't run to me when I came home." His voice wasn't loud. It was low and hard. But he was upset. Angry maybe.

And something amazing happened.

She got angry too. Not scared. Angry.

"I've been here two days. I'm not allowed to leave. I've been living in a basement with no windows for ten years. Never enough food, and water that quenched my thirst only if I wanted the drugs that came with it. You're the nicest man I've encountered in a decade and I'm trying to understand why. Because everybody— *everybody*—wants something." The words flew from her mouth in a quiet tirade that was barely more than a whisper.

And as they did, a funny thing happened. Two things really. One, she felt... *freer*. A bird testing new wings. And two, Ratchet's shoulders lifted and his brow eased. As if he *liked* hearing her mind.

Impossible.

"So just tell me, Ratchet." She squeaked his name and he went ramrod stiff. "What do *you* want from me?"

He seemed to think about it, truly puzzled by the question before he answered, "I want you to trust me."

His words hung in the air while her mind scrambled to make sense of them.

Her lips opened and closed looking for words before she finally muttered the truth. "I can't."

"I know." He let out a breath, running his hand through his hair, frustrated. "Look, can I just... show you the surprise before it's ruined?"

Marlee stared at the paper bag like it held a monster inside.

"Then if you don't like it, we'll try something else. I'll learn what you like. It won't take me long. I pay attention."

She couldn't tear her eyes away from the bag.

"Here." Ratchet held the sweatshirt out to her. "Put this on."

She took it, frowning in confusion as she

pulled it over her head and jabbed her arms into the sleeves.

Ratchet dug in one of the drawers for a pair of socks—two—and quickly jerked one pair onto his feet before kneeling in front of her and unrolling the other.

Her jaw dropped at his actions. What was happening?

He met her gaze and seemed to be asking permission. When she didn't object... because she couldn't fathom what he was doing... he carefully hooked a hand around one ankle, pulling her foot up to rest on his knee.

He was going to put socks on her? Putting clothes on. Not taking them off.

But he just stayed like that, staring at her foot with her messed up nails. Scrapes and cuts that were either scabbing over or still raw. Ratchet brushed his rough thumb over the top of her foot, the gesture seeming... sweet. Soft. Like she craved.

A soft touch.

Like when he'd held her.

She didn't realize how much she needed it. Or how good it could feel. It had been too long since anyone had touched her softly.

She remembered the feel of her mother's hug. But as a teenager, she'd brushed it off so many times, not realizing how much she would long for it again someday.

Now this man touched her softly. And not because she was crying in fear. Not to console her.

It felt... damn good.

"I'm sorry he did this to you." His voice was a rough whisper as he stared down at her foot. But it screamed loud in her ears.

He. It was the way he said... he. Like he knew who had held her for all those years even though she hadn't said a word. It sucked all the good feelings away like a morbid vacuum, and brought the fear back.

Sighing, Ratchet carefully slipped the sock onto her foot and set it back on the floor, then repeated the action with the other one. He stood, digging in a new drawer and coming out with a thick folded blanket. He passed it to Marlee before juggling the paper bag into his arms, and started for the window.

"Wha..." She stared after him. "Where...?"

He slid the pane up, peeking out before he turned back to her.

"There are two fire escapes in this building. This one, and the other on the opposite side. If you go down here, you end up in the lot closest to Felix's door. Don't ever go down, Marlee," he warned.

"Okay." No problem. She didn't want to be anywhere near this Felix.

Ratchet ducked through the opening and held his hand out for her to follow.

"Wait. Where are we going?"

"Up," he said. "To the roof. Come on."

The roof? He was taking her the roof.

She stared at this hand, then found his expectant gaze. He wanted her to come. But why were they going to the roof when she was supposed to be hiding?

"It's safe?"

Ratchet nodded. "Nobody goes up there except me. And there's a light, so it's not too dark."

The roof. Open air. Maybe stars if the city lights didn't drown them out. It sounded magical. It sounded like the tiniest taste of freedom.

Was that what Ratchet was offering her?

Tentatively, she placed her hand in his palm. The feel of his strong grip was good. And even though it was completely new, it didn't scare her, as he helped her out of the window and onto the grate.

With socked feet, they climbed the stairs one level to the top, and Ratchet took her hand again to pull her onto the roof. She clutched the rolled up blanket to her chest as she followed him past the air conditioning units and duct work, mimicking the way he stepped softly.

Socks. So the ones below wouldn't hear them walking. Smart.

They stopped near what looked like a small

utility room. The light attached to the top spread a dim glow over the entire roof.

Ratchet was right. It wasn't dark, but it was dim enough they weren't on display.

Marlee glanced around. She couldn't see the lot. Which meant if anyone came out, they wouldn't see her either.

Ratchet set the bag on the ground and reached for the blanket. She huddled into the sweatshirt, feeling exposed out in the open air.

Would she always be a walking contradiction?

Just minutes ago, this had sounded like a good idea. Now, not so much. She was like a ping pong ball, back and forth. Back and forth. Trying to decide what she needed to feel all right again.

Ratchet unrolled the blanket and spread it on the roof. Then he moved the paper sack to the middle. Like he was setting up a... picnic? He stepped back, hands on his hips, frowning at the scene. They must have identical expressions.

"So... this is it. Your surprise."

He didn't look at her.

"The bag? What's in it?"

"No. Not the bag. This." He swept one arm wide at their surroundings and let it drop to his side. "I thought you might want to get out of the room for a while."

"Oh."

"I come up here to think sometimes. Get away from the clan."

Clan? Is that what they called his little gang?

Marlee moved closer to the blanket, stepping on the edge with her socked feet. It was warmer than the cold metal of the roof.

"There's food," he said, as if that would coax her forward.

Yeah, it worked.

She hadn't noticed before, but now the scent of garlic and cream and baked bread told her the scary paper bag only held dinner. Not something to torture her with.

Kneeling on the blanket, she opened it, peeking in. The wonderful smell wafted out, assaulting her a way she could appreciate.

"Did you make it?"

"No. I will next time. But this will probably be better, because mom made it."

Ratchet crouched beside her, hands hanging loosely over his knees. He managed to make everything he did look rugged. But then the few times he'd touched her, he'd been so very gentle.

Maybe he was a walking contradiction too. Maybe they were more similar than not. Maybe they were even perfectly matched.

She didn't know yet.

But she was going to try and figure it out.

"I like her food," Marlee said as he started pulling containers out, setting them on the blanket.

"Looks like salad and chicken alfredo. You like that?"

She nodded. She hardly had likes anymore. If it was edible and it tasted pretty good, she liked it.

"Yeah. Me too," he murmured. "I get less horny for the salad, but the chicken is fucking delicious. And if we're lucky…" He dug into the bag again, coming out with bottled water and one last rectangle container. "Aw, yeahhhh. Cheesecake. It's the good stuff. Homemade. This is going to make you purr, little lamb."

She stared at him. Was he always so… sexual?

Lamb. He'd called her it a few times.

"Why do you call me that?"

He glanced at her and then back to the food, shrugging one shoulder. "Do you hate it?"

Did she? No. When he used it, it was always sort of… sweet. Like a pet name.

Or did he call every woman lamb?

"Not really," she answered. "But why do you?"

He pulled out the plastic utensils and passed them and one warm container to her, and then busied himself with his own.

"Well… I didn't know your name at first."

Marlee settled in cross-legged and eased the lid off the container, letting the scent of warm food soothe her better than a warm blanket.

"And you looked vulnerable," he muttered.

"Like a lamb. Stuck right in the middle of a den of lions like us."

Vulnerable. She hated being that.

"I'm going to be strong one day."

Ratchet eyed her, stirring his pasta but not eating. "You're already strong. Being vulnerable just means you're helpless. Not weak. There's a difference. It means there are people stronger. Meaner."

And she wasn't that. The years should have made her so. The things she'd endured should have made her leather. A time or two, she'd wanted to be. Mean. She'd wanted to scrape eyes out, and claw skin, and hurt people like she'd been hurt. But the only thing keeping her *her* was her heart. And somehow, she had never let it go black.

Small miracle maybe.

"Stronger then," she said. "One day, I'll be stronger."

He cocked his head, staring at her, and she met him straight on. She wouldn't look away. This was practice. Her being stronger. Every little bit counted.

"I believe you will." His gaze glowed, one side of his mouth turning up in a soft way. It was a stark difference from his snarl, but genuine nonetheless. "One day you'll be the lion instead of the lamb."

His blind faith in her stunned her still. It wrapped around her heart, folding in tight and warming it in a way she'd never felt before.

"You mean it?" she breathed.

Did he really think she could be strong enough to never be a victim again? Because she told herself things like that all the time, because she had to, to make it through the night or to wake up the next day. And maybe she even believed it some, for the very same reasons. But if someone else believed it, that changed everything. It made it real.

If he really believed.

His barely-there smile faded. "I do," he said, dipping his head in a serious nod. "I'm going to help you be stronger, Marlee. You'll see. And I'm not letting anyone hurt you again."

She looked out across the roof, taking in his words and letting them out on a long breath. She wanted to believe them so damn bad. She closed her eyes.

"What if you can't? What if the person is too powerful?"

His long silence made her open again. He looked disturbed, choked even, emotions flickering in every wrinkle of his expression. In the dark, his blue eyes seemed to almost glow.

"Watch and see, female." His voice was gritty, barely sounding human. But like his grip on her neck earlier, it didn't scare her. It soothed her. It sounded like a beautiful promise wrapped in crumpled up paper. "Watch and see what I do if any person tries to harm you."

Again, his words surprised her. Did he mean this too?

But she couldn't ask because in a softer voice, he ordered, "Eat, lamb."

So she ate. Because her stomach had stopped

cramping and jerking. Because her lungs didn't feel like they were breathing through a vise. Because Ratchet was standing guard, and she felt safe.

And he ate too.

They dug into the food, and she tried to remember not to scarf like a starved animal. But no matter how much she tried to slow down and eat like a lady, she ended up with white sauce dribbling down her chin and strands of pasta hanging from her lips.

God. He probably thought she was disgusting.

But why should she care.

Because. You like him.

Even though he wouldn't... or couldn't... let her leave.

Ratchet made a noise that sounded like it was trying to be a laugh. A snicker almost.

Marlee looked up to find him watching her, amused.

"The food's better *if* it ends up in your mouth, lamb." He reached forward, and this time, she didn't pull away. She let him swipe the noodle from her chin with a gentle flick and watched as he brought it to his own lips. He sucked it down, slurping the pasta like a kid would, and somehow... it was the single most intimate thing she'd ever shared with anyone.

How sad was that?

But also, how wonderful.

It was like that movie Lady and the Tramp. Sorta.

Except instead of an alley, they were on a roof.

And instead of red sauce, they had white.

And instead of a lady, she was something else.

And instead of a tramp, he was... what? A savior? He *had* saved her from being found in the shed. He'd given her this little bit of freedom tonight. He hadn't tried to take a thing. Only give.

Maybe... just maybe it was time she started treating him like one, and not like a captor. Maybe if she trusted him a little, he could help her save the others. It was worth a try.

Maybe.

Risky.

She'd think about it.

Thirteen

Ratchet watched as Marlee tucked the empty—and half-empty in her case—food containers back into the bag, making sure she got every utensil and napkin before folding it closed and setting it aside. She liked to keep things tidy, he'd noticed. Probably a habit from being cooped up. Or something she'd done to keep busy. Maybe a little of both.

She sighed and leaned back on her palms to stare up at the sky. The view of the stars wasn't as good as it was out in the country where darkness was thick and black. Here on the fringes of the city, the sky was a deep shade of charcoal, dim night lights peeking through just enough to let you know they were around. But Marlee seemed to enjoy it.

He wondered when she'd last sat like this searching out the stars on a calm night. But he knew the answer. Or close enough. It had been longer than ten years for damn sure.

He watched her, his broken beast loving the content sigh she made. Loving the way her expression was relaxed, not afraid. It transformed her from something already beautiful to extraordinary. Her bow lips didn't make a frown. They tipped up on the sides. Not quite a smile, but enough to make his heart thump double-time in his chest. And her eyes… so green. More so in the dark as she stared upward like she wanted to fly away.

Keep her. Show her you.

But he didn't want her to know who he'd been all these years. He wanted her to know the man he was becoming. The one that would move heaven for her because she was making him a better person.

She has to know both. She has to accept both.

Shit.

Ratchet dug into his pocket retrieving her gift and held it out to her. She stared at it in his fingers, a small line forming between her dark brows. "For you."

She shook her head, lifting her gaze to meet his. "Your marble. You want me to try the toothpaste thing?"

"No. It's for you. To keep. I..."

The longer it stayed in his hands, the worse of an idea it seemed. Why would she want something he'd collected from the garbage? Why would she want anything from him at all?

"I found it today and it reminded me of your eyes. Green like a jewel. So I kept it to bring home for you. Uh..."

Her breath was coming faster as she stared at the marble, wide-eyed. Panic. She was getting afraid again. Shit.

This was too fast. Or... or maybe just the wrong move altogether.

He hadn't thought it through. He collected things all the time. This time, she'd been on his mind, and he'd wanted to share.

"You don't have to keep it," he looked away to keep her from seeing his disappointment. "It's silly."

He closed his hand around it, hurrying to put in back in his pocket.

"No, wait!"

Marlee's arm shot forward to pull his hand into hers. Ratchet froze at her touch. She pried open his fingers until the marble was revealed again, and then just stared.

Didn't let his hand go. Didn't touch the gift. Just stared.

"That's why it was in your pocket. You got this for me?"

He held his breath and gave her a nod.

Her big eyes went to his. "Where?"

He hesitated. What if she didn't get it, the way he searched for treasures in the trash because he needed to find worth in the things people felt had none.

But her little hand cradled his so perfectly and her touch was like catnip to him. He wanted it all over. His hair, his chest, skin, anywhere, everywhere. It made him loose. Made him blurt out the truth.

"To make the days more hopeful I search for treasures in the trash."

She frowned, but not in a way that looked disappointed. More like... intrigued. "Do you find many?"

He relaxed at her question. "Tons. But sometimes they aren't obvious. You have to look hard to see the beautiful parts. This one was easy. Because it's the exact color of your eyes."

She bent to stare at it again, tilting his hand sideways and back to let the thing glisten in the spare light from the security lamp. Her full lips curled at the sides until she was smiling.

"You're right," she whispered, her voice all full of wonder. "It is."

Fucking hell. She was smiling. He'd made her smile.

Shit, now he wanted to kiss it off her face. Yeah, he wanted to do that. Taste it. Test the way it curved around his mouth. Kiss the hell out of her, and see if it was still there when he was finished.

Mine.

She looked up, and he swallowed back the growl in his throat.

"No one's ever given me such a thoughtful gift."

He cleared his throat, trying to brush it off. "No big thing."

She picked up the marble, holding it between her fingers, still smiling as she stared at it. "You do nice things, Ratchet. Why do you?"

He shrugged. "I like you."

It was more than that. So much more. It felt wrong to reduce it to those three words. But how could he tell her all the insane things he was feeling and how much he needed to bond with her?

Careful with mate.

Her hand dropped his. He felt the absence of her touch like a weight in his chest.

Fisting the marble, she stared at him again. "How did you end up here?"

"How did you?" he countered.

"I mean... you're different than the others. I know who the Alley Cats are. Know what you do. That you're organized crime. A mafia of your own, but you work for the king. Do his dirty work. Like everyone in Memphis does."

"You know all that, huh?"

Marlee snapped her mouth shut, realizing she'd revealed too much.

He sighed. "I know he was the one who hurt you. Bastian."

She flinched at the name, and Ratchet fisted his hands to keep from reaching for her. Instead, they both got quiet.

Instinct guided him now. The way it did before the curse. His lamb had to be coaxed. Slowly. He was building trust, and like Rome, it wasn't built in a day.

Even though he really fucking needed it to go up like one of Bastian's shitty office buildings. The construction crew could knock one of those out in three days flat.

Huddling into her sweatshirt, Marlee rubbed the marble between her thumb and finger. Like she was using it to keep calm.

"You know," she murmured to the wind. "Does this mean he's coming for me?"

"Damn well better not be."

Her gaze flipped to him.

"I told you, I won't let him hurt you ever again. I mean it. It's a promise. As real as that marble."

"But he's your boss."

"He doesn't own me. I only answer to my leader. Felix."

"Will he give me up?"

Ratchet dipped his head. "In a heartbeat."

Her shoulders slumped.

"That's why I have to hide you. Just until Felix isn't a danger anymore."

The faintest wisp of hope filled her eyes. "How will that ever happen?"

"He's sick, and getting weaker. There's a change happening in our clan. A storm that will either break us apart or bring us together. Either way, Felix will have to buckle. And me and you, Marlee? We have to wait it out. I don't know what's going to happen, but I can tell you I'm going to make you safe. So safe you'll never worry about anything ever again."

It was a steep promise, but if nobody could muster up any faith for him, he'd have to do it himself.

She stared at him for so long, blinking over and over until he wondered if he'd gone too far.

"I believe you," she murmured. "But I still can't figure out *why*. Why do you want to help me so much?"

But he didn't know how to answer her.

Because you're mine.

No. Too claimy. She hadn't been her own for a while, she wouldn't like being reminded she still wasn't.

Because I need to.

No. Too vague. And there was too much of that between them already.

Because I want to right my wrongs and do one fucking noble thing in my life, and I want that thing to be you.

True, but he wasn't ready to explain his need for redemption yet.

He settled for simple honesty.

"Because something inside is telling me to. And because the idea of you hurting makes me burn on the inside. I'm not a good man. You can see it. I haven't cared about anything in a long damn time, but I care about you. And when something jerks me to attention like that, I'm not in the business of questioning it. I just go with instinct."

"And instinct tells you... what?"

"To be careful with you. To go slow. To give more than I get."

Her eyes went glossy, emotions spilling off them. His girl was so damn expressive. How had that not been worked out of her by her circumstances? How was she able to stay tender, when he'd found it impossible.

"Maybe you're a better man than you think."

He didn't argue with her. She was wrong of course, but he wanted to believe what she said. And maybe someday, really *be* better.

He was trying. He was going to do it. If it took his entire life.

And maybe if he was lucky, Marlee would be next to him when he finally became a good man.

***

Give more than I get.

Marlee couldn't get Ratchet's blunt words out of her mind as she lay on the blanket staring up at the dim stars. They were faded, but still the best night sky she'd seen in years.

Give more than I get.

That was the exact definition of love, wasn't it? Caring more for someone than you cared for yourself. Thinking of them first, even when it didn't benefit you. She'd seen her mother make that choice over and over again. For Marlee. For her father. And it was a fine line, caring for yourself enough to not be taken advantage of. Sure. But it was the purest form of love when another person's well-being mattered more than your own.

The idea that Ratchet might feel that way about her was baffling. It wasn't normal for a person to care that much that fast, was it?

Then again, what did she know about love. She'd been without it for a decade.

He laid beside her, keeping a thin boundary of space between them. Sticking to her rule of no touching. Except she'd broken the rule several times now herself, so it was pretty much moot.

If Ratchet wanted to hurt her, he could. Rule or none.

But he wasn't going to.

She moved her hand along the blanket, a centimeter closer to him. Now that she was convinced he was safe, she couldn't help wanting more of his touch. He was tender with her, and it was like food for her soul. She'd been starved of good things for too long. Smiles, touches that didn't harm, the beauty of the outside world. Now she wanted to gorge on it all until she was so full she couldn't remember being without.

She needed to let him know... what? That she *needed* him? That she took back all that *don't touch me* stuff now that she was trying to trust him.

Closer she moved, until her pinky bumped up against his hot hand, and then she held her breath.

Several moments ticked by. The honk of car horns somewhere below drowned out the thumping of her heart while she waited to see what would happen.

Then Ratchet moved. Carefully, slowly, he curled his pinky around hers.

And that was all.

But it felt more intimate than any kiss could surely.

He didn't ask for more. And even though she wanted more, it was sort of a relief he didn't. She was a ping pong ball again. Needing things and not. Wanting them, then not.

This was good. This was enough for now, pinky holding.

"You never told me how you ended up here." She wanted to know about him. And this is the only way she knew how. It was how she'd started up with the other girls. It was the first question she asked them when they were brought to the basement.

He'd turned away from the sky and she could feel his eyes on her.

"Born here, lamb," he husked. "Born a monster like the rest of them."

"No one is born a monster."

He was quiet. She traced the stars with her eyes.

"You're right. I wasn't born a monster. I just

had one waiting inside me for someone to bring it alive. My father made sure that happened. Along with the other fathers." His breath wisped out the rest. "They taught us how to be cruel. By being cruel. Always."

She thought of the brutal scars on his back.

"They put the S in your back?"

She cringed when he answered, "Yes. And more."

"Who taught you how to be kind?" But she already knew the answer.

When he said nothing, she turned her head to look at him. Their faces were very close but they were still only linked at the pinky.

"Who taught you how to be kind, Ratchet?"

"My mother, I guess. She stayed."

"What do you mean she stayed?"

He blinked, his lashes shielding his eyes, his brow frowning.

"When the other mates left, she stayed, knowing my father would hurt her. She stayed to watch over me instead of leaving me alone with him. Fang, Skittles, Monster, Felix and Gash... so many. Their mothers escaped but left them behind. Mine stayed."

Mates. Funny word to use. It must mean something to his brotherhood. Bastian had his own terminology too. It had taken her years to get it down.

"She's strong, to do that for you."

"For all of us. She was a mother to us all, as good as she could be." He pressed his lips together. "Yeah. She's a strong female."

"She must love you very much."

Ratchet frowned at that. "I think she did once. Then I think it changed to something else."

"To what?"

His breath stalled between them. "Fear," he rasped.

And she could hear the regret in his tone that told him Leah wasn't free here either. But if she was reading his eyes right, he wanted to change that. A storm was coming, he'd said. Changes that would make all the difference.

Ratchet squeezed her pinky with his. "Your turn. Tell me how you became his prisoner."

Her stomach twisted just thinking about it, and she looked back to the stars.

"I was there as payment for somebody's debt."

"Whose?"

She could hardly make the words come out. "My father's. Casino debt. So much of it."

"Shit." His whispered curse gave her strength.

"I thought he'd come for me. Pay what he owed so Bastian would let me go. I was his *daughter*. He was supposed to… to… *care*. But he never came. I was told he said Bastian could keep me. That it made them even."

An angry growl rumbled in Ratchet's throat, but he didn't move. Not a muscle except his pinky.

"My mom tried to find me. Went to the police. Went to the news."

"They did nothing," Ratchet guessed.

"No. Bastian has too many arms in this city. Too many people owe him."

"Did he sell you?" he ground out, his voice doing that gravelly animal sound again.

Tell him the truth. Get it out.

"He tried. Because I had nothing else to offer him. Couldn't hack computers like Nyla or cook meth like Vegas or play arm candy like Skye and Janet. But I refused to use my body to pay off a debt that wasn't mine. Besides..." Her voice got real thin. "I'd only been with one boy in high school and it was awful. Couldn't imagine doing it with strangers. And Bastian said he wasn't in the business of selling his customers a woman who would cry the whole time. That I had to say yes, go willingly, before I could start paying off."

"And you wouldn't?"

She shook her head. "So he started counting. Every morsel of food I ate put me farther in debt. Every bar of soap, scrap of clothing. The heat it took to warm the basement. Blankets I slept on. Pretty soon I was nearly as in debt as my father was. Bastian thought it would convince me, but..."

It had done the opposite. It had made her

want to fight. Not just lie there, his prisoner, but shove back.

"But what?" Ratchet pushed.

Now was the time. She had to lay it out there and see what he'd say. If he really wanted to help her be stronger like he said, then he would help her free the others too.

"It made me tougher. I used only what I needed to stay alive so he couldn't hold any of it over my head. Ate so little I was starving... because one day, somehow, I was getting out of there. Didn't bathe. Slept on the floor without blankets. The girls helped me some. As much as they could without him finding out. And when the time came, they made a way for me to run but only if I did something for them in return."

She turned her face to look at him. Her ear was pressed against the blanket just like his, and her heartbeat thumped hard making every sound seem like it was rolling through a tunnel.

His furious snarl was in place, but she wasn't afraid of it anymore. It steadied her. The way his touch did. Made her feel like with him at her back, she could conquer every demon. If this feeling was real, if it didn't come crashing down in the morning when her eyes opened... if it wasn't a dream like every time before when she'd thought she was free...

Then she was never letting it go.

"The picture," he said, jerking her to attention. "Skittles found a picture in the shed after I found you. Four females. They're the ones who helped you? The other dolls."

She chewed her lip, nodding. "Now they need my help. I was supposed to get far from Memphis, from the people under Bastian's thumb, and then give that photo to the authorities. I didn't make if very far."

Ratchet frowned. "That won't work, lamb. Any rescue would involve local law enforcement. Bastian would be tipped off."

She wilted inside. He was right. With her head clear of the drugs, she should have realized it. But she'd been on a mission and only thinking of completing it.

"I can't leave them there," she whispered.

He pulled her hand up by the pinky, bringing it to his lips while his thunderous gaze held hers. He brushed a kiss there and she felt chills break out all over her skin.

"Give me time, Marlee," he promised. "I'll free them. Free you all. I'll do it for you. I just need time."

She let out a shuddering breath. "Okay."

Silence fell between them, but she couldn't pull her gaze away. And he didn't look away either. Ratchet turned on his side and this put them even closer. Their hands were still linked, nestled between her shoulder and his chest.

"Trust me?"

"Trying to."

He slowly brought his other hand to her cheek, barely touching it with the pad of his thumb. He felt like velvet sliding down her jaw. Rough skin, moving so very carefully. His eyes followed the movement as he paused at the corner of her mouth. Softly pressed in. Like he was testing it.

And she watched his face, the way his eyes flicked between heat and awe. Three heart beats.

And then he took the journey back to her cheekbone, repeating the same exploring touch with the tender skin beneath her eye.

She closed them, letting the breath ease from her body. He was relaxing her. Soul food. Making things inside settle and feel right again. How did he do that?

"You like this?" he whispered. His voice was quiet like he didn't want the night sky to hear him.

"Yes." She kept her eyes closed, not wanting to break the spell.

"Can I touch more?" It came out rough, and again, she got the impression he wasn't used to asking, but he did it just for her. He was used to doing whatever he wanted. "If I'm careful?"

She wanted to say yes. Wanted more of his velvet hands on her sensitive skin.

But she had to know she was in control of

herself. Had to know she could choose, and he would accept it.

She blinked open to find his eyes had softened. He was raw right now. She was too.

Still, she said, "No."

Please be okay. Please don't make me.

Ratchet's hand froze and he frowned hard. "No?"

"No." She held his gaze. He was puzzled. But this was important.

Seconds ticked by. So many. She hardly breathed waiting to see what he'd do.

"But... you do like it?"

"Yes."

His brow eased even if he looked disappointed. "Okay, lamb. I won't touch anymore."

He laid back against the blanket, keeping their pinkies hooked. Her cheek felt cold without his hand there. Bare. Kind of sad. But inside she was soaring.

Her *no* meant something to him. She said it,

and he'd respected it.

It was a test, and he'd passed.

Tears pricked the back of her eyes.

Did he even know what he'd done just now? He'd given her power back. Even if just a little. Even if just when she was with him. She was in charge. She could say *no* and he'd listen.

"Ratchet."

"Yes?"

"I like holding pinkies too."

"Then I'll hold your pinky until you tell me not to."

Fourteen

Ratchet stood in the center of his room, not sure what to do. Marlee was in the shower. She'd taken one while he was at work but insisted on another after they'd climbed down from the roof. He didn't blame her. She was coming from a place where she'd had to save her baths so she wouldn't owe anyone for them.

Bastian was a shitty motherfucker.

Now she wanted to take advantage of her choices.

Ratchet knew she was testing him, and he

didn't mind. He'd show his little lamb all the freedom he could give her until she didn't question him anymore.

He looked around.

He'd fixed the bed, straightening all the sheets until they were crisp, and folded back the big blanket. Fluffed the pillows. Turned all the lights off except the lamp. Set the remote on the side table so she could reach it.

He stared at the floor, then to the chair.

One of those two would be his bed tonight, and he was debating which when the bathroom door opened. Steam rolled out from the crack, but no Marlee.

He frowned, stepping forward.

But then she appeared in the doorway, juggling the used clothes and towels in her arms.

His breath went to hell. She took all his oxygen. Her choppy shoulder-length hair was wet and tousled, and her face was dewy like a rose in the morning—

The fuck?

She made him think the softest things. Dangerous things.

It wasn't that he wanted that to change. It was just... could he afford to be so vulnerable when there was an impending war on the horizon? When he didn't know how to deal with Felix or Bastian or the rest of the cats.

It was a tightrope he was walking. He needed to bond with her and heal, but he needed to be brutal and fierce. Both, in order to protect her.

No wonder his sick animal had withered away.

It takes a new kind to do what needs to be done, the beast murmured.

She dumped the clothes in the laundry basket and yawned.

Shit. Why did that make his middle throb?

Mate needs touch.

No. If she did, she would tell him. It was just his instinct running amok.

Marlee looked up, meeting his gaze with those deep green eyes.

"Ready for bed, lamb?"

She nodded. "I can take the chair this time."

Ratchet snorted.

She blinked.

What the hell.

She wasn't serious. Was she?

"You'll sleep in my bed, Marlee." He wasn't letting his mate sleep anywhere but the best. He was the male, he'd take the less comfortable spot. Unless she wanted to share.

Did she?

Damn, he was out of his element with her. He'd never asked to touch a woman before. Never been told no. And he didn't give one his bed unless he was meeting her in it.

She let you touch her face. Hold her pinky. Worth it.

It was the tiniest victory. It was the hugest victory.

"Where will you sleep?"

He shrugged one shoulder. Jutted his chin toward the chair he'd thought was pretty damn comfortable until last night.

"Okay." She moved toward the bed. Did she sound the littlest bit disappointed?

She climbed in and he pulled the covers up to her chin.

"You'd make a good dad," she murmured.

Fuck.

A dad? The only one he had turned him into a monster. And... she didn't know a good one either. No. Being a father wasn't in his future. His mom thought that's what he wanted from Marlee, but she was off.

"Strong and safe," she slurred.

And if Marlee was thinking of him like a father, he was doing things all wrong. He wanted her needing him, the way he was needing her.

No sex.

Yeah, he'd set that boundary. But that didn't mean he wanted her thinking of him like a father figure. And he wasn't so sure his new animal was on board with the stipulation.

Bond, his inner beast insisted. *Listen to her*

*heart, what it says to you. When she's ready, mate.
Mark. Claim.*

When. His beast said when. As if she would be
ready eventually. And he wanted to believe that.
He wanted in that bed with her. Wanted her in his
arms so bad his throat ached. Wanted to feel her
small body shielded safely by his while they slept.

But it was probably for the best.

The way his animal churned inside for her...
it left him with a semi-constant hard-on. She
made a fire inside him. Hot until he touched her.
Then he went cool. Like she was the balm for
whatever burned away at him. At times, he
wondered if he'd turn to ash. But her little looks,
touches, they cooled him enough he didn't.

Was this how Malcom had felt when his curse
burned away? And how long did it take?

He'd ask, but the cat wasn't taking his phone
calls.

"Night, mate," he rasped, but she was already
dozing off.

He settled into the chair, kicking his feet up

on the edge of the bed so his long legs were almost touching hers. There. He was a little closer this way. It was enough to fool his animal. Or maybe just his mind. Whatever.

"My bed, my mate," he grumbled. "Chair's just fine."

She let off a snore and his scowl softened.

His girl slept so peacefully under his watch. Meant she was trusting him.

He'd sleep in a chair every day for the rest of his life for the feeling that gave him. More satisfaction than burying himself in her body. Because this meant he was winning her heart. And maybe that never meant anything to him before, but it did now. With her.

He fell asleep basking in it. Fell hard, and slept like the dead. Better than he had in years. Until he woke to Marlee's terror-filled scream.

Ratchet fought his way out of the deepest slumber, dragging his eyes open to find his mate still asleep in the bed. She thrashed and kicked, whimpering, "No, no."

A nightmare.

"Marlee."

He didn't think about what he was doing. He flew out of the chair, kneeling beside her on the bed. Her head moved side to side, tears rolling from her closed eyes. He put his hands on her cheeks, brushing her hair away and held her.

"Marlee. Wake up," he urged.

Her eyes snapped open, looking glassy and confused. And scared.

"Lamb?"

Was he too close? Was she okay? Was she awake or still stuck in the dream?

"Ratchet?" Her voice was hopeful and soaked with tears.

"Yeah, lamb. I'm here. It's over. Just a dream."

She blinked again and again, leftover tears still rolling. "I was back in the basement," she whispered. "Trapped. Alone."

Ratchet shook his head, thumbs brushing each of her cheeks. "You're not there. You're here. Not alone. With me."

She nodded quickly, like she was trying to convince her body what her mind knew was true.

"Safe," he rumbled, continuing to pet her cheeks to calm her. "Safe."

They were close. They were touching. He didn't know if it was the right thing but his new beast was purring a fiery approval in his chest. And he watched his mate closely looking for signs she wanted him to back off.

"Safe," she repeated, her voice not even making a sound.

Seconds ticked off and he could feel her panic retreating. But shit, he didn't want to pull away. Not when her cry had rattled him out of sleep. His animal was fired up and ready to go. Ready to fight or…

Fuck.

Would she let him hold her? Just that much?

"Ratchet?"

"Hmm?"

"Will you… can you… um…"

"Anything," he growled. "Name it." He stared

into her eyes trying to understand what she needed.

"Stay?" she blurted, and then clamped her mouth shut. Like it had escaped unwillingly.

"Stay."

She nodded. But what did that mean? He wasn't going anywhere.

"In... in the bed. Here. While I sleep. Can you?"

Can he? Fuck, it was all he'd been wanting.

He nodded, and her breath rushed out in relief.

He eased to the bed, stretching his body out beside her, trying not to touch more than the mattress made him. Even though everything inside him was demanding touch. He damn near needed the comfort as much as she did. Soon, she would have to let him closer.

For both their sakes.

But hell, he was so rough. Could he do things right with her? Take his time, be gentle.

He didn't think he could.

He was a thorn, she was a petal. The two were

kept apart for a reason.

But no longer, his beast purred. *Now the fire makes new, and mate makes clean.*

The thing was like a fucking fortune cookie. Maybe one day it would all make sense.

Marlee turned on her side to face him. She inched closer, pulling the covers up. It made them seem even closer. He could smell her sweet scent. Wanted to lick it from her skin. Pick a spot and just go at it. Until her taste and her smell were so entwined that he couldn't tell them apart.

He stared at her neck. It looked soft. But he'd only touched the back. He wanted to feel the front. Wrap his palm around her throat. Squeeze just a little to show her he was in control and to prove to himself he could be careful.

Kiss her jaw.

Whisper something in her ear that only she would ever hear.

Swallow her gasp as he kissed her.

Pray that she moaned when his hands wandered, feeling her small curves.

Shit. The bed was a bad, bad idea.

Ratchet clenched his jaw, his breath sawing in and out of his lungs.

He could do this. Hold it together for her.

"Ratchet," she whispered.

He found her gaze and tried to strangle his desire. He couldn't let her see that he was close to snapping—

"You can touch me."

"No, lamb." His throat was rocks. "I can't."

"Earlier you wanted to."

He swallowed hard. "It's not that I don't want to. I want to too much."

"Then what's the problem?" Her voice still quivered from leftover adrenaline.

"Don't want to scare you," he admitted.

"You haven't yet."

But she hadn't seen him crazed with lust. Because he'd never felt it this strong before. He wouldn't risk hurting their fledgling bond and pushing her away.

"I want it," she whispered. "You calm me."

Mmm. That drove him even hotter.

She was doing the opposite of calming him. She was building a fire so hot he was afraid he'd explode. And since he didn't know what was happening inside his body, no way was he putting her in the middle of the blast.

But there was something he could do. It would make them both feel better. Hell, that was putting it lightly. It would make him feel like a fucking king.

If she'd let him… he was going to make her come on his hand.

If his mate would give him that much, it would quell the fire. Just giving her pleasure. He knew it.

"You sure?" He was going to ask once. Just once. Give her one chance to take it back. And then he wasn't asking again. Because his beast couldn't keep holding back his nature. He was dominant. And Marlee would have to accept him like that.

Eventually.

"I'm sure."

He searched her eyes. There was no trepidation. Had he really won her enough for this?

There was only one way to find out.

He pulled Marlee into his arms, watching her reaction. Eyes wide. Scared, but not of him.

Scared of her feelings.

Me too, little lamb. Me too.

He slipped his hand up the back of her shirt, smoothing his rough palm along her spine and pressing her into his chest. She fit there just fine. Perfectly even. The perfect shape to patch the hole in his heart.

She snuggled closer, and he breathed through the fiery pounding of his heart.

Was he getting hotter? Damn.

"This good?" he strained out.

She nodded against his chest. He traced his thumb over her shoulder blades, his fingers over the small bones of her back. Her little nails pressed into the fabric of his t-shirt. She wasn't used to good touching. It reminded him of when he was a cub. If not for his mother, he'd never have known the difference between a punch and a kiss.

Right now, he was going to remind Marlee the difference between the good and the bad.

Dragging his hand to her waist, he squeezed, waited, letting her get used to his hands on her.

He was taming her. Taking all the fight out of her so she could save it for when she needed it. Taming his mate. While she made him feel wilder than he ever had.

He played with the waist of the sweatpants she wore. He was going to have her order some new clothes online tomorrow. She'd like that. He knew she was bare underneath, but he kept from going straight for her ass. Instead, he swept up her ribs, feeling the way her breath hitched as he went higher. He paused with his thumb just under her breast.

Ask.

But he didn't want to. He wanted to *tell.*

He settled for somewhere in the middle.

"I'm going to make you feel good, lamb. You say stop, I will. Understand?"

"Yes." Her whispered breath hit his neck making him flush all over.

Shit, the fire burned.

Sliding his hand up, he palmed her tit, feeling her small nipple bead against his grip. She gasped, going tense against him.

Wait. Slow. Easy.

This was why he couldn't fuck her. He could never go easy with her, and that's what she needed. But he could do this. Touch. Touch her until she was quivering with pleasure.

He only moved his thumb, sweeping it over the swell of her breast until her breath came back.

"Stop?" he asked.

"No," she whispered.

And inside his beast roared a victory.

He squeezed her softly, demanding his bastard hand be gentle. So far, so good. And moved to press his hand to her sternum, feeling her heart pump in her chest. His middle finger dipped into the hollow beneath her throat and she swallowed instinctively before he dragged his hand down her flat stomach to the front of her sweats.

Her breath was coming in short pants now. Her fingers pulled so hard at his shirt the collar was tight.

"Ratchet?"

"Hmm?"

"Why are we doing this?"

"Because we need to bond, my female. This is the way. Very carefully."

"I don't understand."

"I know. Just feel me."

She swallowed hard. "I do. I like it," she admitted, and he found her face. It was flushed red, making her green eyes pop in the dim lamp light.

"Good," he growled out.

His cock was hard as steel, barely confined by his jeans. He was glad he'd left the button undone to give it some room. Because he wasn't taking the thing out. Marlee trusted him, but he didn't trust himself. And he wasn't grinding it against her hip. He was keeping the throbbing thing a goddamn secret as long as he could, even though she must know what this was doing to him.

He slipped his fingers past her waistband, probing all her soft flesh until he found the cleft of her pussy.

And that's where he stopped.

Because Marlee had pulled his shirt so tight she was damn near strangling him. And her teeth bit her bottom lip so hard she was about to draw blood from the part of it that was split. And her face was turning crimson from the breath she was holding.

"Breathe, baby," he ordered.

She exhaled in a rush, gasping in more air and holding it.

She shook in his hold and he hadn't even touched her there yet.

Holy shit. Was she that close to coming already?

His beast purred inside. Perfect little female. So responsive to his touch even after all the ugly things she'd endured.

But he knew how she felt. He could feel his heartbeat pounding in his dick. One pump and he'd be done, but sacrificing that for her right now made him feel ten feet tall and invincible.

"Stop?" he asked one last time.

"Nm hmm," she whimpered.

Good mate.

Soft as a feather, he slipped his fingers through her folds, groaning at the slick wetness there. A rush of satisfaction rolled through him. A tidal wave starting in his chest and ending at his crotch. Fuck.

"Marlee," he groaned. "Your body likes my touch too."

She clamped her thighs tight around his hand, breath heaving.

He dropped a trembling kiss to her temple. The first. But definitely not the last. "S'okay. Won't hurt you. Never."

She nodded, twitching and gripping his shirt like it was her lifeline.

"Open up and let me feel you, baby. Trust me."

She inched her legs apart. Not much, but when she did, Ratchet eased his finger farther inside, slicking along her lips until he bumped against the tight little pearl of her clit.

She jerked at the contact even though it was hardly more than a breath.

"Ratchet! I... I..."

Oh, his name from her sweet mouth when she was about to tip over the edge of pleasure... it was all he could take. He pushed his hips into the mattress, feeling the sting of his brutal erection, the tightening of his balls...

Again, he slipped his finger through her wet cunt.

"Scream, moan, cry. I don't care," he rumbled, resisting the urge to nip the shell of her ear. "Just give me what we both need, mate. Come apart on my hand. Feel good. I need you to feel *good*."

Damn it, he did.

Felt like he'd never find oxygen until she was pleasured. Until she had completely forgotten about her nightmare, and all she knew was him.

With a sweet little gasp, she rattled apart, twitching and writhing so perfectly. His cock jerked in response, his release pounding through him as he came harder than he ever had in his life.

Sweet fuck.

Sweet fucking hell.

Inside, his beast burned and roared. The thing was growing stronger. Like whatever he and Marlee had just shared gave it strength.

Her breath raced. His did too. As they came down from their high, and he couldn't free his hand because her legs had it in a vise.

He imagined what those thighs would feel like gripping his hips the same way.

A few more breaths and she eased her hold on him. He pulled free, bringing his finger to his mouth to lick her orgasm from it. It was as close as he was getting to actually licking *her*, and it wasn't nearly good enough. But it was a start.

He tamped down the feral snarl in his throat at her taste. *Mine.* If there was ever any doubt, it was flown out the window, sailing five hundred yards over Kentucky by now.

Mine.

"Wh-what now?" Marlee breathed.

He met her gaze, knowing his eyes must be showing some of his new beast. She watched wide-eyed as he licked his finger again, making sure to get every drop of her essence.

He pulled her into the circle of his arms, unable to stop himself from dropping another kiss to her forehead. But she was soft in his hold, not rigid. They were good, and he felt amazing. Nearly whole.

Nearly.

"Now you sleep. And no more nightmares, lamb. Because I'm here. Watching over you."

Fifteen

Marlee paced the small bathroom, waiting for Ratchet to get home. He was late, but not much. Just enough that it was getting dark and she'd come into the bathroom so she could turn on the light.

She wondered how much longer she'd have to pretend she didn't exist.

Ratchet wanted her to give him time. He would help her free the girls but he needed time. Well he'd had almost two weeks, but they were no closer to a rescue attempt.

It hadn't been a bad two weeks with him. In fact, just the opposite. She'd gotten to know him. Seen his tender side so many times, she finally understood what Leah had meant that first day.

He knows how to be right. He just needs to remember.

Ratchet was a good man. Or... he was *now*.

His past was questionable. But he was trying so damn hard to make up for it. She could see that.

And his careful ways had gone a million miles to helping her heal.

Everyday, Ratchet left her in his room and went to work. Each day he brought her a new gift he'd found. Little sweet gestures that had seemed weird at first.

A dragonfly brooch that was rusted and missing most of its gemstones. He said to remind her of the Dragonfly Inn from "Guillotine" Girls.

An eraser shaped like a slice of chocolate cake. The very tip had been used but it was mostly there. He said, to remind her of her first meal as a free woman. She didn't have the heart to remind him she still wasn't free yet.

A bottle cap. Whiteish plastic. Like from a bottle of drinking water. This one had meant a lot, she could tell by the way he'd given it to her. He had stood so still, so quiet, as he held it in his palm for her to take. Shoulders high, like he was proud.

"To remind you I'll always give you unopened water so you know it's safe."

He'd cleared his throat like his words hadn't come through right, and tried again.

"To remind you I won't do things that make you feel unsafe. No matter how strange it seems."

He'd frowned, opening his mouth to try again. But she got the message.

He would change the paint color in his room if it made her feel better. Remove the rug from the floor and hang it over the window. Line all his socks up on the dresser instead of inside it. Whatever.

She had lunged at him for the second time, wrapping her arms around his waist and pressing her cheek to his chest. "I love it," she had whispered against his grimy shirt as he'd curled his big arms around her again. And she relished the touch, the safety, just like she had the first time.

He was determined to do right by her. And she didn't always understand why. But his effort stole her heart. He said cryptic things like that they were 'growing a bond' or that she was his 'mate'. Or like last night when they were lying in bed falling asleep, and he said, "You're giving me back my life, lamb." He'd squeezed her a little too hard, but she hadn't complained because she liked how strong he was. It made her feel protected. Like she had her very own bodyguard. "Do you know how amazing you are?"

Every night, they took to the roof so she could get air. She kept expecting him to kiss her. Or repeat what they'd shared the one time in his bed. Expected more of those magical touches that made her feel like she was flying and wiped every ugly part of her past away, even if just for a few minutes.

But he'd mostly held her pinky. Only in bed or when she greeted him at the door, would he wrap her in his arms and hold her like she wanted.

Yeah. She wanted that. And even more.

It was unbelievable that her heart was opening like this. Unfathomable. And if anyone had asked her weeks ago if she'd ever feel safe enough to be close to a man, the answer would've been a hard no.

But Ratchet made her stronger. Gave her power she thought she'd never have.

And hope that one day she'd be completely free.

She paused as she heard the bedroom door open, and her heart did a ridiculous flip, making her want to grin.

He was home.

She reached for the handle, but before she could turn it she heard a voice she didn't recognize. And double as many footsteps as there should be.

"Ratchet, you in there?" The voice belonged to

a man and wasn't familiar. It had the same rough edge as Ratchet's, but not nearly as patient.

Marlee went cold.

There was a stranger in Ratchet's room. What if they opened the bathroom and found her here?

Fear slammed her in the chest, grabbing hold of her throat to keep her from breathing.

"We need to talk about this picture, asshole," a second voice grumbled, also male.

Picture. Was this Skittles? The man who found the photo she'd dropped in the shed?

"Can't fucking take it," the first guy said. "Gotta get the females free or I'm gonna go batshit fucking crazy. Deal with the consequences later."

A heavy hand pounded on the bathroom door, drawing a surprised gasp from her as she stumbled backward and crashed into the counter. Her foot hit the trash can, scooting it across the floor. The sound was thunderous in her ears.

Damn it.

She was preparing for one of them to come through the door when Ratchet's booming voice covered up the noise she'd made.

"The *fuck* are you doing in my room?" He was furious. She'd never heard him like this. Rough, on edge, sure. But livid? Ready to raze the place? Never.

"Shit," the first voice said. "We thought you were in the bathroom. Chill the fuck out."

"Look," the second voice said low. "Felix is gone for a few minutes, and we wanted to discuss our little problem."

Silence stretched out, and Marlee held her breath.

"What do you want?" Ratchet demanded.

"We need a plan. We need to get these females away from Bastian so we can heal our animals. Whatever this thing is inside me is shredding me all up. Won't stop until I get her out of there."

Animals. What animals? And how could the other girls help them.

The calmer one—Skittles?—spoke up. "I agree. We need to act soon. We don't know what kind of hell they're in right now. What if we wait too long? What if... if..." He faded off on a growl that sent chills down Marlee's spine.

"Look," Ratchet said, irritated. "I know. I want to get them free too, but I called Malcom. He won't talk to me. If you got a plan, I'd love to hear it. Otherwise, you need to get out of my fucking room."

There was another long silence.

"Why?" the first voice asked.

"Why? Because I'm tired and I need a shower, and don't want to look at your face when I don't have to."

He was trying to get them out of the room to keep her cover.

"No. Why do you want to free the girls? What's in it for you?"

More silence. This time she could swear she felt a crackle of energy through the door.

"You got someone in there?" the second voice asked. "Who's in the bathroom, Ratchet?"

"Nobody," he ground out, and somehow it

sounded like a threat.

"Light's on."

"Left it on this morning."

"Sure about that?"

"Dead fucking."

First voice spoke up again. "You never answered my question."

"You're asking me why those females in the picture matter to me?"

"Yes."

More silence.

"To break the curse the witches put on us, we have to change. In our hearts. Do right, and not wrong. Help, not hurt. Isn't that what they said? I want my animal back just as badly as anyone. If that means freeing a few females that aren't mine from a bastard I don't like, then that's what I'll do."

Seconds ticked on and Marlee tried to make sense of what Ratchet told the others. A witch put a curse on them? A witch. Like from *The Craft*? Okay. And what was the talk about animals? Was this some Alley Cat code?

"Okay," the calmer one said. "Fine. Here's what we were thinking. The females are somewhere on Bastian's compound. Monster thinks we need to get one of us on the inside. Find a reason to get close. Maybe work a security detail, if we can get the Junkyard Dogs to give up one of theirs. Then we find the girls, and break 'em out. Don't go in all guns blazing. Infiltrate instead. Do this stealthy."

"It could work," the first voice agreed.

"We have to be careful," Ratchet warned. "If Felix finds out, we'll have the entire clan against us."

"Let me worry about that," second voice said, and she heard boots moving toward the bedroom door. "We'll talk tomorrow on the route. I got us all on the same truck again. Deal?"

Ratchet must have nodded, because seconds later, she heard the door slam shut. And then silence.

Hope fluttered in Marlee's chest. Maybe the girls would be free faster than she'd thought. At least these two from Ratchet's clan were on board. Desperate even, though she didn't understand why yet. What was their stake in this? What had them turning against their boss for a few unwanted and forgotten girls like her?

It was a problem for later.

Right now, she was just happy someone was fighting for them.

It seemed like an eternity before he opened the bathroom door, and leaned against the jamb like he was working to keep his distance and the frame was holding him there.

"Hi," he said.

"Hi."

"You okay?"

She nodded. "That was a close call. Are they dangerous?"

"Yes."

She changed her question. "Would they hurt me?"

His full lips dipped at the corners while he considered it. "I don't know, lamb. But I'm not taking that chance. From now on, that door stays locked. Shit, they know better than to come into my territory."

He was still angry. Furious. She could see it in the way he stood, the snarl on his lips, the way his words came hard. She'd only ever seen him angry once before, that first night in the lounge.

She took a step closer. Instinct told her if she could touch him, she could tame that anger. Get him back to being her Ratchet.

"Stay back, Marlee," he rasped. "You heard what we said about the animals inside us."

Was he talking about his crimes? His dark past. The gang life had made him an animal? Taken his humanity and forced him to be cold? Because if that was it, she wasn't concerned. She'd already seen his heart, and it was good.

She took another step.

Not just because he needed her near and she could sense it, but because she needed the touch too. The fear of getting caught was still fresh in her veins. And that adrenaline threatened to toss her stomach. She knew Ratchet could make it better. Like he'd done before.

Magical.

In the doorway, he straightened. "I'm not steady right now. The beast inside me wants to do things to you."

"What things?"

"Things that will make you *mine*," he said darkly.

Marlee froze.

His. It should have crippled her with fear, the idea that she wasn't her own. But it didn't. It lit her up inside. Made her achy and needy for him. Like she'd been the night he made her come so hard. He'd damn near healed all the holes in her heart that night. The way he only *gave* when everyone else—anyone else—would have *taken*.

It didn't make sense, really. It was just fact.

No matter what happened between them in the future, she would always have a spot in her heart that only belonged to him. The man who gave more than he got.

She swallowed hard, giving him the rest of herself with two words.

"Do it."

His entire expression crumbled like a brick wall taking a wrecking ball. He shook his head.

"I want that," she said, lifting her chin.

His eyebrows shot up before falling back into the harshest frown. He threw off dominance like he was his own hurricane. She resisted the urge to step back, out of the storm. But the eye was where the calm was. Right in the center of him, that's where she'd find peace. So she stepped forward.

"You want me to claim you? Put my mark on you?"

More of that code talk. Had to be. Because he couldn't be talking about *actually* holding an animal inside his body. That would mean he was some otherworldly creature—or partly anyway—and she didn't believe in the supernatural. Real life was scary enough.

Magic though, the way fate worked, the way two people's spirits could call to each other... she believed in that.

"I want you to heal me."

"Marlee…"

"Do it. Fix me. I know you can. You've been doing it little by little this whole time. I feel it. The thing inside me trying to connect broken pieces. You call it a bond."

"There are other ways," he argued. "We don't have to… I don't have to… *take* you."

She swallowed back her fear and focused on the burning desire in her center. It was growing into a consuming fire. Her mind fogged with lust at just the idea of him working her body into the kind of frenzy that she'd felt with just his finger.

"Give more than you get. Right?"

"Yes," he grit out.

Well, she was amending that.

"Then *take* what is given. Because it means a hell of a lot when it's given freely."

His eyes flared hot. Did that thing that gave her chills. Like pure desire showing straight through those soul windows.

"No, no, no," he breathed, pumping his fists. "Can't have you, Marlee. Can't risk you. Can't hurt you."

"It wouldn't hurt. Not with you. You can show me how."

He looked tortured, his face contorting as if in pain. "I'm not gentle," he rasped.

"You can be."

He shook his head.

"When you hold me, you do it so easy. So careful. When you touch my skin, it's with your fingertips. Like I'm..." Her voice cut out. "Like I'm precious." She mouthed the words, unable to say them out loud.

Her throat ached. Everything inside throbbed. She felt like if he said no she'd shatter to tiny pieces. She needed this. For him to take all the horrors of the past decade and erase them the way he had her nightmares. There was magic to him. She didn't understand it, but it was real.

He shook his head, some battle raging inside. "You'll regret me. You'll..."

"Please!" she cried. And damn it, she could feel the wetness under her lids. The moment was heavy with what this would mean for them. "Don't say no. I need this. Put... put me back together."

He crowded her slowly, but she let him. His shaking hands brushed her hair back, and trembling so hard, he cradled her cheek. "Okay. Okay, lamb. I can be soft for you."

It sounded like a promise. And it came from somewhere deep. Like he'd just made a decision about her. Them. The future. Something.

"I'm going to kiss you," he warned. "Tell me when you want me to stop."

She shivered, her body trembling with anticipation.

"What if I never want you to?" she whispered.

Ratchet groaned. "You're fucking killing me, lamb. Do you know how hard I want to take you?"

His thumb swept over her cheek, still gentle, but his fingers dug into her jaw letting her know he was barely holding back.

"How I want to master every part of your

body until it knows me so well you go all wet when I so much as *breathe* on you."

Slowly, a hand slid around her waist, fingers splayed wide like he was trying to increase contact, touch her as many places as possible with one sweep, before coming to stop on her lower back, his middle finger resting at the top of her crack.

"Wanna make you moan those sweet whimpers you made the first time you let me touch you. Because fuck, baby... I've been aching to hear those again. But how am I supposed to go easy when you're saying things like this? Hm?"

Marlee chugged for oxygen. Even gentle, Ratchet was intense.

"You'll find a way," she managed. Because this was it. She was giving him all.

He dipped his head, brushing lips over hers in a sweeping motion as he backed her into the bathroom, stopping just as her butt hit the counter. He licked at the seam of her lips, begging for entrance. It was so soft she went liquid.

Turned right to mush with him holding her. Melted good, and all she could think about was what his soft, capable tongue would feel like *down there.*

She opened with a gasp and he pressed in, swirling his tongue with hers. They danced. Softly, tentatively. And she took the lead for a second, wanting him to go harder. Wanting more of him. She could hardly remember how to kiss, but she hoped he liked what she was doing.

He pulled back with a hard suck to her bottom lip, his mouth glistening wet from what they'd done. His breath washed over her face making chills break out all over her skin.

"Goddamn it," he husked. "Your kiss is so fucking sweet, lamb. Never had a kiss that sweet. Making my fucking knees weak, and I thought that was all bullshit. You're going to be sweet all over, aren't you? Sweet tits for me to suck. Sweet ass for me to bite. Sweet pussy for me to lick." He groaned, taking her mouth again. Softly again. Like this was new to him, and he loved new things.

While her heart thundered at his blunt words and she moaned into his mouth.

How did he make dirty talk sound like poetry?

He pulled back, brow furrowed as he stared at her chest hungrily. A beast wanting to devour and savor at the same time. Like he was debating the fastest but least frightening way of getting her shirt off.

How was a man like this, rough and wounded and hard, this thoughtful?

But the answer was screaming through her mind already, pounding in the hollow of her chest. *Because he cares. He's different with you because he loves you.*

She solved the problem for him by lifting the shirt over her head and tossing it to the floor, leaving her completely exposed. Leftover bruises, scars, and all.

And she held her breath.

Ratchet stared, his eyes going lusty as he moved his hand over curves, hovering just over her skin but not touching. She felt it though, chills rocketing up her spine.

"Mine," he said, and she gave him a nod that felt so right.

When his touch finally made contact with her skin it was like an electric shock, drawing another moan from her lips. He grazed up her stomach, over her sternum, avoiding her breasts until he reached her throat. Softly, he curved his hand around it, his thumb pressing in under her jaw. His eyes snapped up to hers, asking a question. Or... demanding something.

Trust.

She swallowed, holding very still. And he didn't squeeze. He just kept his hand there. A test. Which she must have passed because he dove in for another lush kiss.

And then his hands were all over her. Gentle and probing, squeezing. Nails scraping. Callouses making desire pool wet and hot between her legs.

Ratchet lowered his head to her collarbone, licking and nipping it with the soft pads of his lips.

Nothing hurt. It only felt good. Soul food times a zillion.

She watched, panting as he went lower, giving her breast the same treatment before he sucked her hard nipple into his mouth making her cry out. Her hands flew to his hair, tangling in the blond tresses until he looked up at her.

His eyes looked feral, staring at her, his mouth still sucking and lapping at her sensitive bud. She couldn't look away. They were locked as his hand continued roaming her body, feeling every uncovered part of her.

He tugged at her pants until the front was low enough for him to touch her like he had before. He slipped one finger between her slick folds, using the waistband to keep the pressure there as he moved back and forth against her clit. Which felt like it was on fire and he had the only way of extinguishing it.

Damn it though. He was talented. He never even stopped sucking her.

Could she be enough for him like she was?

She pulled at his shirt, needing to feel his skin, the strong muscles he held in check to make her comfortable.

Maybe he didn't need to do that anymore. Maybe she was strong enough to meet him halfway.

But he slid out of her grasp, going to his knees between her legs and sliding her pants all the way down and off her feet.

"I like you not wearing panties. Never wear panties again."

"Mmmm." She'd agree to almost anything right now. And panties were an extravagance she'd done without for too long anyway.

He gripped her hips and pressed his nose just under her belly button, dragging downward on a long inhale. He exhaled a deep groan and continued over to the crease of her thigh, breathing her in.

"Love your scent. My animal loves it too. Even better after it's mixed with mine."

Marlee shivered. It was such a carnal thing to

say. She… *liked* it.

"Up on the counter," he commanded.

She scooted her butt up, ignoring the cold surface. Were they doing this in here? Did she care where they were? No. Not really.

But before she could say anything, he palmed her thighs, spreading her legs wide and gave a slow, soft lick up her center.

A gasp shot from her throat causing her to choke on her own breath. Holy hell. Oh god. That was even better than she could have imagined.

She both felt and heard Ratchet's hungry snarl against her tender flesh as he threw her legs up over his broad shoulders and settled in. He sucked and lapped at her, thrusting with his tongue, every motion making her suck in too much air until she felt lightheaded.

Her palm hit the surface of the surface of the counter with a smack and her hips bucked against his mouth as she spiraled out of control, her release hitting her harder than a wrecking ball and doing just as much damage.

"Can't breathe," she wheezed. "Can't... can't..."

Ratchet stood, his expression looking wicked. Like he'd meant to ruin her lungs. He let off a low growl that sounded anything but human, but the way his arms circled her reminded her who he was. Protective, careful Ratchet.

"Mmm, I felt you come undone on my mouth, lamb. Tasted it. Last chance to say no."

He found her gaze. His seemed to glow. If fire could be blue that would be his eyes.

She found enough breath to hiss, "Yessss." *More.* If her body needed oxygen it could just faint or something.

Ratchet pulled his shirt over his head in one smooth jerk, and shook his hair back from his face.

Lion.

The word whispered through her mind.

He reminded her of a lion. Fierce and deadly, but somehow soft for his lamb.

He never took his eyes off her as he undid his

belt with sharp motions. And then his button...
and the zipper. He let his jeans fall down his hips,
gripping his huge erection in his fist.

Marlee stared down at it. God, it was thick.
What would that feel like deep inside? She
wondered if he'd let her do what he just did to her.
She wanted to taste.

"Touch it, Marlee," he groaned.

She wrapped her fingers around him. He was
scalding hot and smooth. "Like this?"

"Fuck. Perfect," he huffed. Good. She was
taking his breath away too.

She ran her hand along his length. Up and
then back down.

"Last chance," he reminded.

"I want you." Did she ever. She was sawing
her knees against his hips wanting more.

His gaze went soft and he kissed her. A noise
in his throat that reminded her of purring, had her
feeling wild.

He slipped his hardness up and down her
folds like a sweet warning about the invasion she

was about to get.

He pushed in slowly, watching their connection while she panted through the sensations. He stretched her to the point of pain, but she didn't want to give up. So when he pulled back too soon, she let off a volley of unintelligible objections.

"Shh. You're tight, baby. Can't hurt you. Gotta be slow. Gotta be careful this time." His words were short, muttered like a mantra he was determined to follow.

In and out, he moved, making progress with each stroke until he was buried completely inside her and both of them were sweating with the effort of holding back. He held her close, letting her body get used to him. But she was already so close to her next orgasm, her muscles were clenching on him.

She moved her hips to urge him on, and he got the message. Inching out and pressing back in, watching her face the whole time.

"I never wanted anyone like you, like this. Soft

like this. Never until you." He held her hips, grinding in and out, bringing her closer with each push. "And now I want you slow, fast, hard, sore, again and again, a million ways. Every morning, every night. I'm never going to want to stop, lamb. Look what you're doing to me."

But he would if she told him to. And that was why she trusted him. Why she... *cared* for him. Loved him?

"Don't want you to stop," she breathed against his cheek, and he moved faster at her words.

"You say the sweetest... fucking... things," he grunted with each push.

And the farther they went, the more patched up her past became. Until it felt like a bad memory. One she could turn her back on, and forget as she moved forward.

There was hope. Maybe it was silly, but with every reminder of their physical connection, Bastian and his cruel ways faded to the background. And in his place, was the reality that she could make something beautiful of her stolen life. Starting now. All she had to do was try. Fight back against the ones who wanted to hurt her. Cling to the ones who didn't. And face her fears like Ratchet showed her.

"More," she whispered, digging her nails into his shoulder, and throwing her head back to feel his mouth on her neck.

"Fucking beautiful, Marlee," he murmured, measured thrusts pushing her forward. "That's what you are. So damn beautiful like this."

Another drag and push of his body in hers was all she could take. She cried out as pleasure wracked her body making every nerve ending vibrate. She was shaking apart from the inside and Ratchet didn't stop. Didn't rush. He kept his slow pace dragging out every wicked sensation, making her feel like this orgasm would never end.

And then with a satisfied growl, she felt him explode, hot jets pumping inside her. Emotions battered her, so many she couldn't sort them out. But the strongest of them was... *good*.

This was what feeling good—truly *good*—was like. And Ratchet had given it to her.

Somehow, she was going to pay him back for it.

This time, not because she owed anyone. But because she wanted to.

Because she was *choosing* to.

Her choice. For the first time ever.

Sixteen

Ratchet lifted his mate from the counter and walked with her to the bed. He was still inside her, still connected and desperately didn't want to leave her warmth. What if this was it. What if this was the only time he'd feel her like this.

She was limp against him, her head tucked into his neck where she breathed hard trying to recover.

Shit.

He was shaking to pieces inside. What had he just done? How much damage. He'd been careful, hadn't he? Careful enough? He didn't know.

He'd put her in bed and find out. Check her over. Every inch. Look into her eyes and make sure their bond was still intact.

Mine, mine, mine, the beast roared.

The thing was angry he hadn't claimed Marlee. Marked her. But there was no way to do that without the animal part of him fully intact. No claw to pierce her skin. No scent marker to give her.

And still, he wouldn't have done it until he was sure she was ready for him. Her choice. He would never force anything on her like his father had his mother.

Gooood. Keep mate safe. Especially her heart.

The beast settled, and Ratchet set Marlee on the bed, slipping free of her body. She rolled onto her side, tucking her face into her hands.

Fuck.

Was she crying?

He stood frozen beside the bed, unable to move as that fear washed over him. The fear he felt in the shed. Fear of hurting her.

"Lamb," he croaked. *Please*... shit.

She shifted, moving her hands enough to peek through her fingers. But he didn't see any tears.

She moved her hands more to reveal a smile like nothing he'd ever seen.

She was smiling. Grinning ear to fucking ear. Teeth showing. Eyes glowing. She was shining like a goddamn angel or something. So pretty when she was happy.

Happy. He'd made his Marlee happy.

Fuck him.

His breath rushed out as relief slammed his chest.

"You smiling?" He crawled up the bed to her.

"Think so," she said, but the grin didn't fade.

It was still there.

He was going to kiss it.

He pounced on her, straddling her waist and pressing his mouth to her lips. A bit harder than he had the first time. He was going to kiss her everyday, as many times as he could get away with.

But she didn't stop smiling. Even better, a laugh bubbled up and he pulled back to watch her. Inside, his beast purred his approval. Claiming would come later. If he could make his lamb do this, he could do anything. He was feeling invincible, pride wanting to burst out of his chest.

Her hand came up to touch his face, her fingers tracing his lips, his forehead, the scruff of his cheeks.

"No scowl," she murmured, eyes still twinkling. "No snarl."

He shook his head, soaking in every bit of her expression. He wanted this marked in his mind forever, the way she looked right now.

"No fear," he whispered, tracing her smile with the tip of his finger. "No sadness."

"I liked that almost as good as pinky holding."

Bullshit. She liked it better. "Pinky holding didn't make you smile."

"Okay, fine. This was better than pinky holding. But... did you? Like it?"

He rolled to the side, pulling her with him, crushing her against his chest and then easing up when she winced.

Careful. Still must be careful.

"Like it? No, lamb. I didn't *like* it. There's no word for what this was to me. I... shit, I... woman, I want to keep you. Understand?"

Her thin arm squeezed his waist, her head nestling into his chest.

"Wanna keep you, Marlee," he repeated quieter. "Lost everything I didn't hide. Every treasure was a vulnerability. Clan found it, clan destroyed it. And now I want to keep you more than any of those."

He couldn't see her face, but he knew her smile was fading away.

"I'm not trying to leave."

It relieved him. It bothered him.

"You should be. They almost found you today."

"You wouldn't let them hurt me."

That familiar fire rose in his chest at just the

idea.

"I would have tried. But I'm not sure I could have stopped them. And Marlee... they would hurt you to get to the other dolls. Without hesitation, they would have."

She stiffened. "What do they want with them?"

"The same thing I want with you."

"Softness to ease the hard things done to you? Someone to look after. Someone to talk to at night when you come home from work. Someone to make the bad things seem less bad. To make the future seem brighter?"

"Yes," he rasped. "And more."

"What more?"

"They want to fall in love."

Marlee went quiet. Ratchet reached for her hand, looping his pinky around hers.

"Why would they want that? Isn't it a vulnerability?"

"Not for my people. It will fix what's broken inside us."

"Your animal."

He stared down at her. How to explain this…

"The dark parts inside, you think finding love will fix you."

He nodded. That was the simple version.

"What happens when the girls are free and they don't want to be here?"

Was she asking for herself? Did she want to leave still? He wanted to make her free, give her everything, but he couldn't. She was hiding in his tiny room with only the roof for freedom at night.

"I don't know," he admitted. He couldn't guess what Skittles and Monster would do with their females. "But I know they won't hurt them. If there was ever a question, I wouldn't let them anywhere near your people."

"How do you know?"

"Because…" He kissed her hair, whispering the rest to her. "You being hurt scared me more than anything had in a long, long time. And it took me fucking three seconds to realize that."

She shivered, pressing in tighter.

"I see the way Skittles carries that picture around. Like it's his girl and not just a piece of paper. He feels it. He won't hurt her."

Silence fell over them, and he focused on her breathing. Normal. Easy. She wasn't scared.

"I think they would choose this," she said eventually. "If given the choice to be Bastian's dolls or be here... even locked away... I think they'd choose this. Because I would. I have."

Instinct pushed him to do better for her. To make her happy all the time, instead of just a few minutes of the day.

"You won't always be locked away," he promised. "I'll find a way, lamb. You'll see."

He only needed the firecat, then he'd give her the entire world.

***

Leah froze just inside her office. The walls were feather-thin and Felix was in the one next door. His booming voice wasn't as strong as it could be, but it was loud enough for her to hear everything he was saying even with the doors closed.

"You telling me you lost one of your girls? Is that what you're saying. Because who gives a fuck, Bastian. Just go out and find another one. Shit. Why are you bothering me with this?"

The clock on the wall ticked off the seconds while she held her breath, not wanting to miss a detail of this conversation.

Because her gut was telling her this was trouble.

"No, I ain't seen her. And I'm not in the business of hunting, okay? Trash. I take out the fucking trash. You got a body you need disposed of? That's what my guys do. What we *don't* do is recovery missions. Especially when she's been missing two weeks. Damn, she's probably long gone by now. Cut your losses."

Bastian was looking for a woman who went missing around the time Marlee showed up.

Shit. Was that sweet broken girl Bastian's?

Her stomach took a floor dive.

"What the hell, asshole.," Felix continued.

"You know I don't kill females."

That was mostly true. At least it was true for his reign as Alley Cat leader.

"If you want her dead, go ask the dogs. Though, I bet they'll tell you the same thing. This is stupid. So she turns up at a PD somewhere. You got enough of them under your thumb for a cover up."

If Marlee was who Bastian was looking for, she was in trouble. Major trouble. She needed to get out of Memphis.

"Don't throw money at me, dickwad," Felix fumed. "I don't need it."

But the clan did. And whatever faults Felix had, he took his job looking out for his people seriously.

"How much?" Felix's voice was dark and angry. He hacked out a vicious cough they were all becoming familiar with. Leah wondered how much longer he could make it without his animal.

"Motherfucker."

Chills ran down her spine. This wasn't good.

Not good at all.

You didn't mess with the Lord of Memphis. Not unless you wanted to be dead.

She pressed her lips together to stifle a sob.

Thomas. Her boy could end up dead over this.

"Fine. Shit, fine. Okay? I'll hunt her down. For every penny of that. But I'm not killing her. You'll have to find someone else to do that."

He slammed down the phone making Leah jump at the sound. One, two, three...

Since the beginning when she first fell in with the Alley Cats, one rule kept her going. Made her move forward when she wanted to cower. It was the rule that had kept her alive. Kept her son alive, and it would do the same thing now.

She gave herself three breaths to be scared. Three breaths to feel the terror this life inflicted at any given time.

Three breaths only.

And then she did whatever she needed to, to keep the one who mattered safe.

Thomas. He was all she had, and all that

mattered.

That meant Marlee had to go. Not just away. But back to Bastian.

She pressed her palms into the desk leaning forward to force blood to her head. Deep breaths. No tears.

Damn it. She didn't hurt females, she saved them. So many of them.

Her stomach twisted. This wouldn't end well. Not for her, not for Marlee. But Thomas would be alive. Bastian wouldn't kill him for taking his property.

Shit. Property. Women weren't property.

Everything she'd worked to protect for so many years... she was about to throw it all away with this betrayal.

How would she live with herself? How could she ever look at her son again?

Her gut clenched and she dove for the trashcan, heaving until her stomach was empty.

Boots thumped across the floor, stopping just beside her.

"Mama Kitty?" It was Skittles. "You okay?"

Her gaze followed his legs up, past his leather vest, the bright colored tattoos covering his arms and neck to find his scowling face. Skittles was the heart of the clan. He just didn't know it yet.

And if he didn't know it... she could use him.

No! Shit. Don't do it.

She had no animal, no werecat, to guide her. She only had her conscience. And it wouldn't recover from this decision.

Leah battled back her tears, tipped her chin forward.

For Thomas.

"I need you to do something for me," she choked.

He squatted beside her, hands hanging over his knees. "What do you need, Mama?"

As if in slow motion, a slip of paper fluttered from his vest to the concrete floor. She reached for it, and he stiffened. It was a photo. Four unsmiling females in a dim room.

"What's this?"

He shrugged, pulling it from her hand. "Just something I found in the shed."

"The shed?"

Where Marlee was.

He nodded.

The dolls, Marlee called them. Her captor had five dolls. This picture was Marlee's. It meant Skittles was onto her. And it meant Bastian was one good luck move away from finding her here. And finding out one of his own had betrayed him.

Thomas was about to be exposed.

They had to move fast.

Seventeen

Marlee pressed up on her tiptoes to kiss Ratchet. He liked making her work for it, but he could only hold off a second or two before he took over. It made her grin. She liked him desperate for her.

He wrapped his thick arm around her waist, one hand threading into her hair to hold her for his lips.

Like she'd pull away now.

She'd been waiting for him to get home all day. Waiting to see if his kiss was as amazing as she remembered from the night before.

It was. Maybe even more so.

He lapped at her, still so careful. Still holding back.

Burying his face in her neck, he breathed deep. "Fucking missed you, lamb."

She clung to his neck, breathing in his fresh scent mixed with the ash she always smelled after he got off work.

"Looks like you missed me too," he whispered when she didn't want to let go.

Whatever. She didn't like being alone, so him coming back was like a freaking Christmas present every time.

Speaking of presents.

She leaned away. "What did you bring me?"

His eyes twinkled even with his scowl in place and the sexy twist of his lips. "Nothing good enough for you today. But I have a different surprise for you."

He took her pinky and pulled her toward the closet. From the top shelf, he pulled a black laptop computer. He set it on the dresser and plugged it in, opened the lid, and booted it up.

"What are we doing?" she asked.

"We're going to see what happened to your father?"

"Why?"

"Because I want to kill him for what he put you through."

His blunt words pulled a gasp from her. He couldn't be serious. Or maybe he was. She knew his clan was fierce. Otherwise why would Bastian depend on them for bad things.

Either way, it didn't much matter.

"I already know what happened to him."

She told him how her father died. How Bastian showed her the newspaper article, with pictures of the knife.

"Oh." Ratchet frowned, looking even more bothered.

"Are you disappointed?"

"Yes. I wanted to be the one to kill him."

She shoved his shoulder gently, murmuring,

"You can't just go around killing people."

"I can if they hurt you." He said it like it was law. If a person hurts someone you care for, you have the right to end their life.

"It's kind of against the law," she reminded.

He shrugged like he didn't see the problem. But she needed him to. Bastian might deserve to die, but when they went to save the others, she couldn't have Ratchet going to jail and leaving her to deal with his crew alone. She didn't trust Skittles or Monster or anyone but him.

"No killing people, Ratchet," she tried, unable to keep her voice from shaking. Not exactly the authoritative tone she'd hoped for.

She wasn't his boss, but he seemed to listen to her. When he asked her opinion, and she gave it, it meant something. Just like her *no* had that first night on the roof. He considered her feelings.

But he seemed troubled by her demand.

"Mate, we will negotiate on this."

Okay. She jutted her chin. She didn't know how to negotiate with a man like Ratchet, but she'd stepped up. So it was either back down or keep going.

"No killing people who are nice to you." He seemed satisfied with his amendment.

Marlee shook her head. Was she really doing this? Standing up to this big bad man... who was not so big and bad with her?

It made her feel... powerful.

That was the thing about him. He never let her feel weak.

"Fine." He frowned. "No killing people who are nice to you and who don't hurt you... from now on out."

"Meaning, you can kill people who have hurt me in the past?"

He dipped his head in a nod, his hair casting shadows over his cheeks to make him look brutal. Like when he found her in the shed.

But he wasn't brutal, was he.

No. He was.

He was exactly the kind of brutal she needed. A warrior. Who would stand and fight for her, be her shield, be her conqueror. Because she'd been in the fiercest battle for most of her life, and she'd been standing alone.

But no more.

"Why do you need to kill the ones from my past?"

"Because. They deserve to die."

Boy, did they ever. Especially if they intended on hurting anyone else. But that wasn't real life. It wasn't the way the world worked. Maybe the world never worked the way it should.

"Nobody ever gets what they deserve, do they? If they did, I wouldn't have ended up Bastian's prisoner. You wouldn't have gotten your back cut up. Your mother wouldn't have become part of this gang..."

He narrowed his eyes. "I wouldn't have you." He said it quiet, like what she was saying made sense to him.

She waited while he worked it out in his mind.

"How should he be punished then? Bastian?"

She thought about it. Like she'd been doing

for so many years. It was part of what kept her sane, thinking about what she'd do to him if she ever got the chance.

"My wish..." Her voice went wispy, and she pulled on some of her new-found strength to get the rest out. "... is to destroy him."

Ratchet nodded, eyes sparking like he'd pulled her over to the dark side. Damn. Didn't he know she already lived there? His 'little lamb' might be timid, but she'd been through enough to make her ruthless when she needed to be.

"Destroy him, and then make him live with what he's done. Live with the consequences. Live with the misery, the guilt, if he's even capable of it. Isn't that the worst kind of punishment anyway?"

He dipped his head solemnly. "It can be."

Her voice was thread-thin. So small, but it didn't matter. Ratchet was listening. "I want him poor and starving like I was. Cold and aching. Lonely. Bitter. But most of all? I want it impossible for him to hurt anyone else again. Ever."

Realization dawned in Ratchet's gaze as he stared down at her, and she knew her version of Bastian's punishment was more ping pong ball thinking. Because the only way to ensure he could never hurt anyone was to kill him.

"Okay then, lamb. No killing people unless they are Bastian... and as long as they are nice to you."

She pressed her lips together. It was probably the best deal she was getting. And besides, Ratchet wasn't wrong on this.

"Fine."

A look of satisfaction spread across his face. "Now that that's settled. Is there anyone else you want to find on here?" He slid the chair over for her to sit in front of the computer.

"My mom," she whispered. "I'd like to know how she is. Where she is. Because when it's all over and the girls are safe, I want to see her. But... you know, not until the nightmare is over. Really over. I want to bring her smiles, not more to worry about."

"Type her name in."

Marlee clicked around a few seconds, trying to get her bearings. But the internet had changed a lot in ten years. "Uh... here?"

"No, there."

"Here?"

"No. There."

"Right here."

Ratchet sighed. "Stand up."

She let him have the chair and moved to stand behind him. But she didn't get very far because he pulled her down onto his lap.

She froze in surprise, but he just squinted at the screen and moved the mouse around like a pro. His other arm linked around her waist like it was natural, like they sat like this all the time, his hand resting on her thigh while he worked.

"Name?"

"Uh... Gina Miranda Benson. Her last address was 2014 Penn Avenue."

He tapped it out in the box and hit enter. Her eyes scanned the results as he scrolled, and it didn't take long to learn a new horrible truth.

"Marlee," he said, going tense. "She's—"

"It's not her."

No way. It couldn't be.

His arm tightened around her waist as he clicked the link for a news article from three years ago.

Her mouth went dry as she read the headline:

Mother of Teen Missing Seven Years Dies Without Answers

"No," she breathed.

But her eyes were scanning ahead. They hit on the words 'cancer' and 'broken heart' and 'local Casino mogul Bastian Marx'.

She slowed down to read, but her eyes were filling with tears, and her heart was begging this to be a mistake.

Marlee Benson, eighteen, disappeared mysteriously seven years ago, walking home from a movie late one Saturday night. Suspicion was cast by family members on a local casino mogul with known ties to her father. After a lengthy investigation, Bastian Marx was cleared as a person of interest, leading police to look more closely at her father as a suspect. Which also resulted in a deadend when he died in 2011. Now, after a lengthy battle with cancer, her mother Gina, has also succumbed without ever having closure in her daughter's case. With no other leads, the world may never know what happened to young Marlee Benson.

"No. No, no."

She could feel Ratchet watching her, his grip on her tightening, but she couldn't stop reading about her mom dying, sick and alone, and still believing Marlee was alive and being tortured for her father's debts.

Emotions pelted her like some angry hailstorm. She felt faint. A hand flew to her chest where her heart was breaking.

This wasn't supposed to happen. Not this.

She'd dreamed of the day when she was free. And part of that dream had been showing up on her mother's doorstep. Knocking on the door.

Anticipating her answer. Seeing the look of relief on her face as she was reunited with her only daughter. Feeling her mom's arms wrap her up in a hug like she used to do when Marlee was a kid.

And now...

After all that. After fighting so hard. She was never going to see her mother again.

If only she could have gotten free sooner.

But how? Three years ago, before Nyla came, she'd been in even worse shape than when Ratchet found her.

Mom, no.

Cancer. She'd died from that beast. Died knowing she would never find out what happened to Marlee.

It was too much. This was too unfair. How much horrible shit did the universe have waiting for her? How much was she supposed to endure?

A sob burst from her throat, and she didn't try to stop it. She succumbed. Because if there had been any little bit of hope that her life could be righted eventually, it was dust in the wind now.

Bastian had truly taken every part of who she used to be from her.

Now there was only what she would become. And she wasn't sure what that was going to look like.

Your name is Marlee Benson...
Fill in the blank.

***

Ratchet watched his mate from his perch on the blanket. They'd taken to the roof even though it was just barely dusk. Marlee had needed air, and now she was pacing a dent in the metal roof.

Three days had passed since she learned about her mother. Three days of her tucking away back into herself. Three gifts he'd brought home that didn't light up her eyes. Three nights of holding her through nightmares.

They were moving backwards.

And if they kept it up, he'd never be strong enough to protect her. Nevermind the entire clan.

Enough was enough.

He got to his feet, standing in her path so

she'd have to stop and face him.

"Talk to me, mate."

She came to a stop too far away but at least she met his gaze. "About what?"

"Whatever has you a mess right now. I can feel you... *tortured* over something. Feel it through our bond."

He rubbed at his chest, the burning spot there in the center. It was getting hotter but that's as far as it went. And the more hopeless she felt, the more he was beginning to believe their situation was doomed.

Shit.

"What does that even mean?" she snapped. "Why do you talk in code?"

He frowned. "Not talking in code. I'm trying to tell you I feel what you're going through. In my chest. I just don't know why. And if I don't know why, I can't fix it."

"Maybe you can't." Her voice flew at him all high pitched and panicky. Like it had been before.

Yeah, they were definitely moving

backwards.

Fuck.

"*Come here*," he growled.

She lifted her chin, arms crossed over her perfect little chest. "No."

No?

Oh, he wasn't taking no for an answer.

"Marlee, come here."

"Why?"

"Because you need to be reminded."

"Of what?"

Goddamn it. So many questions. And this sassy side of her was turning him on.

What was he thinking? Every side of her turned him on.

"*Of who I am*," he snapped. "Of what I can do for you. Of how far I will go to get you back to how you were a few nights ago. Happy and safe. Like you should be."

Her mouth fished open and shut, and all the fight bled from her expression.

"Come here, lamb," he demanded softly, and

this time she moved closer.

"I'm sorry," she whispered, tears wetting her eyes. "I know you're trying."

Fucking tears. He hated them. Especially after making her smile so much.

"I won't stop," he promised. He swiped one away from her cheek. And another. One more before curving his fingers around her jaw. "Tell me."

"I just keep thinking, if I could have gotten free sooner, if I'd worked like Bastian wanted... I could have paid off the debt and... and... *been there for her.*"

The tears came too fast for him to wipe away.

Shit. His lamb was stronger than he ever knew. But she was down right now. Hurting in a way he couldn't fix.

"But that's not all. Then I think what if the same thing is happening to one of the girls? What if every day that I'm here, every day I don't get help for them, is keeping them away from someone who loves them. Someone who needs them. All of this swirls around inside me until I feel sick from it, Ratchet. We have to do something."

"I know."

He pulled her into his chest, finding relief in the way she leaned on him. He couldn't let her down. She was depending on him to free the girls. So were Skittles and Monster. But the beast inside wasn't giving him any more. The healing had stalled after he took Marlee to bed. Almost like the thing was confused.

Inside, he was changed. A brand new man. One who could love and felt loved. But he was no closer to shifting. He couldn't form fire like Monster. And there was no roaring, flame spitting beast pushing out of his body like Malcom.

And without the beast... he couldn't keep Marlee safe.

His gut clenched at the implication. He'd promised her protection. Even from himself. Even from his clan.

He swallowed hard, fingers digging into her

hips to keep her near.

If he couldn't get his power back, the only way to make her safe was to send her far away from the Alley Cats and Bastian. Far away from Memphis. So far that none of them could ever find her.

No, the beast roared. *Keep her. And keep the young. Keep ours.*

Ratchet went stiff at the words rolling through his mind on repeat.

Keep her.

Keep the young.

Keep ours.

Young. What young?

He pulled back to look at her. She was the same. No change. He heard wrong. Or... his beast was losing it. Going insane from being broken so long.

"What?" she asked. "What is it?"

Mate is with young. She carries a cub.

No way. No fucking way.

He bent his head to her neck just under her

ear, inhaling hard. Again and again, desperate for confirmation.

"Ratchet, what are you doing?"

"Scenting," he said distractedly. But no matter how much of her scent he pulled in, he couldn't smell a pregnancy.

He went to his knees, spreading his fingers over her flat stomach. He couldn't feel the energy that should be there. The little flare of light behind her skin telling him there was a new life growing. He couldn't feel anything like that.

"Ratchet?"

His senses were too dull. They weren't as dull as when he was first cursed, but they weren't healed enough to sense a young. Or fertility, he realized. Goddamn. How did he miss that? *Of course* he couldn't smell her heat like this, without his cat.

Broken.

Not completely, the beast reminded.

Half healed, still useless.

He lifted her shirt, pressing his nose to her

skin and inhaling again. And then lower, closer to her—

He froze.

Arousal.

Mate is needy.

"Ratchet, please. Why are you doing this?"

But if he could smell her need, he could catch some hint of a baby. He just had to keep trying.

Come on, you fucking firecat. Give me something.

He tugged the front of her pants down, exposing her hot pussy. She gasped at his actions but didn't stop him. Gripping her ass, he pressed her hips to his face, dragging in so much air he felt lightheaded.

And there it was.

The faintest hint that her essence had changed. So faint, it was a fucking miracle he could sense it at all.

He inhaled again, just to be sure.

Young. She had a young in her. One he'd put there. Damn, he hadn't meant to, but now the idea filled him with so much satisfaction he was practically bursting.

Satisfaction and... *fear*.

He couldn't keep them safe. Not her, and especially not a baby.

Not from Felix and the Alley Cat life. Not from Bastian. Not from... himself.

"Fuck."

He stood, somehow keeping his feet under him.

"Ratchet?" Her question came out a half-moan. Her eyes were lusty and beautiful.

But he had to tell her.

"Oh shit, Marlee. *Shit*. I think I put a baby in you."

She blinked. It must have been twenty times. The lust evaporated like fog meeting the morning sun.

"*What?*"

"A baby, lamb. I think I gave you a baby."

"H-how do you know?"

"I can smell it. When was your last heat?"

She blinked again. "My *heat*? Ratchet this is crazy. Are you... are you okay?"

Shit, what did the humans call it? "Your cycle. Are you late?"

She swallowed hard. "My period? I haven't been normal for a long time. It went away when Bastian kept food from me. It only came back once or twice in the past year. I... I... don't know."

He hooked her pinky and pulled her toward the ladder. He went down first, landing on the grate with a thud before reaching up to help her.

Careful. There's a young now.

When she was on the last step, he lifted her down and helped her through the window. He pulled her to the bed and motioned for her to sit.

"Stay there. Do not move. I'll be back."

"Where are you going?"

"To get a test."

He kissed her head and stalked for the door, but she stopped him before he made it through.

"Ratchet?"

"Yeah, lamb." He found her worried gaze and

did his best to push strength to her through their bond. Their bond that was feeling shaky instead of strong.

"I'm scared."

"I know." And fuck, he couldn't stop his next words. "I am too."

Then he pushed into the hall, emotion making him burn.

And this time there would be nothing to put the fire out.

Eighteen

Marlee sat on the bed, feeling bewildered. Cradled in her hand was the proof that Ratchet could freaking *smell* a pregnancy. She stared at the white plastic strip and the two little blue lines still feeling like this was one big prank. Or another stupid dream. Would she wake up and find this wasn't reality?

But no. She knew it was real.

She'd taken the entire three pack of tests.

"Say something, mate." He stood in the door of the bathroom, rigid, arms crossed.

Scowl in place.

Damn. She loved him, didn't she? Like, really loved him. The man who gave more than he got.

Except this time he'd given her something they would share forever.

"How did you know?"

"I could sense it." As if that explained knowing she was pregnant before she did.

"But... *how*?"

He pushed off from the jamb and began pacing. "My animal," he muttered. "It's in there, and it knew."

He glanced her way, seeing she was still confused and tried again.

"I have a beast inside. It's hard to explain. The thing has been broken for a long time, but it's healing now, since you. Since finding you and loving you. You, you, you. Shit, lamb. I told you... you're everything."

"I don't understand."

He stalked forward, falling to his knees next to the bed. Her buried his face in her stomach again, inhaling hard. But this time he didn't seem like a bloodhound. More like he was trying to keep it for remembering later. He squeezed her close, nuzzling his cheek against her like a cat rubbing on its human.

Something was wrong.

She could feel it in her middle. That piece of her heart that had pulled her toward him since the moment he found her... it *hurt*.

"It doesn't matter anymore. Explaining what I am isn't important after this," he said, exhaling a shuddering breath. "There's only one thing that matters and it's that I can't protect you here. I can't keep you and a young safe."

She set the pregnancy test aside and hugged his head close, running her finger over his hair. Whatever that did, his arms tightened around her even more. Anything to make him feel better. They could get through this. Sure, they could.

They just needed a way to beat Bastian. A way to make Felix a nicer person.

Or maybe that's what Ratchet meant. That

they couldn't stay here. Not now, with a baby coming.

Okay.

They could run away. It would take longer to get the girls free now, but they would find a way.

There was always a way.

She nodded to herself, tangling her fingers in his hair. She'd lost hope for a minute after learning about her mom. A sharp ache hit her chest at the reminder. But she was Marlee Benson. She'd survived being Thirteen. She'd found a way out, and now she'd find a way through the rest. She wouldn't stop until everyone she cared about was safe.

"What now?" she asked, pressing her lips to his head. He'd know what to do. He took such good care of her. Always. He'd be the most protective father for their baby. Be hard, because it was who he was. But he'd be soft too, because that's what he wanted for the people he loved.

His arms got impossibly tighter, his fingers digging into her flesh.

"Now..." His voice was gritty. He didn't sound like himself. And whatever solution she'd expected him to come up with, it wasn't what came out of his mouth. "It's time to set you free."

"What?" She frowned and pushed his head back until he looked at her.

His expression was twisted like in pain. And there was no doubt that his eyes had changed to something else. The blue blazed so bright she was sure she'd be able to see them in the dark.

"Time for you to be free, lamb," he growled low. "You need to leave tonight. Get far from here. Take our baby and live a good life. One where there's no reason to be afraid. One like you deserve."

"What?" Things inside were crumbling, the bottom sliding out of her world all over again. Like it had so many times before.

"You have to go. I'll stay here and finish what we started. Free the dolls, heal my clan." His gaze went dark. "Make sure Bastian can never hurt you or anyone else again. This is how I make you free,

Marlee. This is how I make sure my young is never raised an Alley Cat."

"No," she snapped, pushing him away. She shoved him hard, palms smacking against his chest. He got to his feet, hands in the air like he was just going to take whatever else she threw. "No. I'm staying."

"It's too dangerous," he hissed. "You're a vulnerability."

The word snapped from his mouth like a slap. And it stung as bad as one.

"You said love wasn't a vulnerability for your people," she shot back. "That it could heal you and change you and make you stronger." But her voice sounded hurt instead of angry like she wanted to be.

Ratchet looked away, shaking his head. Sadness poured off him. His fists clenched. "Not this time, lamb. It wasn't enough."

Shit.

Knife. To the chest.

God, she knew she was broken. But he had

accepted her like that. Wanted to put her back together.

"I wasn't enough?" she squeaked.

His head snapped around and he looked furious. Mad enough to punch a tree. She imagined that's what he would look like when he finally killed Bastian.

"No, mate. *Me.* I wasn't enough. I can't bring the firecat out, no matter how much I love you."

What the hell was the firecat? Enough with the code.

"And without it, I'll never be enough to keep you safe. I have too many enemies and so do you. And now... there's another life to think of. You have to leave. And I have to let you go." He closed the distance between them, tucking his knuckle under her chin to bring her eyes to his. "Set you free."

Freedom. He was giving it to her but now she didn't want it. What she wanted was a choice.

And she still didn't have that.

Maybe she never would.

"I don't want to do this alone. Be alone. I want to be with you. You make me feel good things. I'm not walking away from that."

Ratchet looped his pinky around hers, and pulled her up to his chest. His big palm settled over her belly where a new life grew. One she already felt protective over.

"You have to, lamb," he said.

And she knew he was right. Whatever was to happen in the future, *right now*, she had to protect the innocent life they had created. Until Bastian was no longer a threat, and the Alley Cats' cruel world shifted...

She had no choice.

***

Leah's hands shook as she hung up with her son and hurried to dial Skittles' number. The ring of the phone sounded like betrayal.

"Yeah." Skittles sounded distracted.

"We need to do this now. She's ready."

"And Ratchet? He away?" His voice got quiet. "Because if he finds out I'm doing this, he'll have my balls on a skewer. Shit, worse than that."

"He's letting her go. Wants her gone. And he won't know you're helping. I'll get her out and meet you at the shed."

There was a long silence. So long she almost pulled back her phone to see if the call had dropped.

"Bullshit, Mama," he hissed. "He'd never let her just leave."

"He called me. I didn't even have to convince him. He's letting her go, and he's trusting me to get her out safely."

Her stomach twisted. Was she really doing this? Giving Marlee back to the vilest of men.

Skittles hadn't batted an eye at helping her. He was doing what was good for the clan, giving Marlee back. A second in command through and through. She didn't know what she'd expected, but the tiniest resistance would have at least let her know the witches' curse on her boys was doing its job.

"You still with me?" she asked, half hoping he

said no.

Because if he said yes... Leah was going to betray her heart in the worst way.

For Thomas, she reminded herself.

A long sigh came through the phone. "Yeah, fine. Meet in ten."

"We'll be there."

"Oh, Mama?"

"Yeah."

"Not the shed. Meet me out by the trucks. Back row, got it?"

"Got it."

She hung up the phone feeling dirtier than she ever had. She hoped this was worth it.

Because she was going straight to hell.

Nineteen

Ratchet examined the contents of the duffle bag one more time. He had packed Marlee's clothes, an extra sweatshirt of his, all her treasures he'd brought her over the past weeks, a pocket knife, whatever portable food he could scavenge from the kitchen... water...

Fuck.

Some bathroom items, a flashlight...

Goddamn it.

The wad of cash he'd stashed in the hole in his closet wall.

Shit.

He was trying hard not to break anything. When Marlee was gone, he'd do enough of that. He'd punch a hundred holes in the walls just to remind him what his fucking heart would look like without her around.

He looked over at her. She stared at the bed, her eyes looking numb. The green not so brilliant. She hugged his t-shirt—the one she wore that first night—to her chin.

His chest locked up.

Who would hold her when she had a bad dream in the middle of the night? Who would make sure there was always a light for her when it was dark? Or turn on Glimmer Girls when she couldn't sleep?

Maybe he shouldn't let her leave. Maybe—

Keep mate safe, the beast growled. *Young too*.

It had taken a battle like nothing he'd ever fought to convince himself this was the only way. The beast didn't want it. The human didn't want it. But both knew it was necessary.

The wounds of that war, were hidden inside and he'd never recover from them.

At least he hadn't marked Marlee. Now she could go on, and have a life without him. Without feeling like her heart was ripped from her chest. And she wouldn't find her way back to him. There'd be no mating bond to draw her back. Not after this.

It would fade for her.

But never for him.

Just as well. He was done with females. He'd found his. He was letting her go. And there'd be no other. Ever.

He forced his feet over to her, tugging the shirt from her grip and adding it to the bag.

"Smells like you," she murmured.

He nodded stiffly. His throat ached with holding back tears he didn't even know he could cry anymore.

"Keep it, lamb."

"Do... do you want something of mine? T-To remember?"

The whole fucking room, the roof, chicken pasta, the goddamn chair. It was all a memory of *her*. He didn't need anything to remember her by. She was emblazoned on his fucking heart. She'd branded him. He wouldn't take one breath in this room without smelling her.

But he answered, "Yeah," anyway.

She rushed forward, ripping the bag out of his hands and rummaging through it. When she found what she was looking for, she took his hand and set the reminder in the middle of his palm.

A green jewel-toned marble. The exact color of her eyes. With a couple scratched up places that could probably be fixed with toothpaste.

Ratchet couldn't take his eyes off hers as she closed his fingers around it and whispered, "So you don't forget."

"No chance of that, lamb. Not ever."

She gave a brave watery smile. Weak, but it was there. "Maybe after things are safer we can be together again. After—"

The knock at the door interrupted her.

Melting the smile into tears.

Ratchet pulled her forward by her neck, pressing urgent kisses to her face. "Gonna be okay," he forced out. "You can do this, Marlee. You are strong. So strong." He, on the other hand, was going to crumble to shit when she was gone.

Another knock had him pulling away to fumble with the lock of the door. He cracked it open and his mom slipped in, shutting it behind her.

"Ready for this?" she asked, and he noticed the nervous shake to her voice.

Ratchet nodded. "You sure taking her out the front is the best plan?"

"Yes. Everyone is in the lounge. I can get her through the offices and out of the warehouse."

"Okay. And you'll drive her straight to the bus station, right? And don't leave until she's on the bus. And watch for the bus to pull out of the station. And—"

"I got it, son," she assured. "I know exactly what to do."

Her eyes went to Marlee, and Ratchet saw sadness there. His mom was getting what she'd wanted from the beginning though. She'd told him he would have to let Marlee go.

She was right.

"You ready, hun?" Her voice shook. And why did that set him on edge?

Ratchet shook it off, and went to his mate. One last time, he knelt before her, pulling her belly to his cheek.

Last time. Say goodbye.

He kissed her there, not caring that his mom saw him like this. Broken like this.

"Be healthy," he whispered. "And when you're old enough, look out for your mama. She doesn't like the dark. So you be the light. Make her smile sometimes. Or lots of times. For me, okay? And... don't let anyone ever take your skin. Don't let them make you hard. Yeah... okay."

He hugged her close, feeling her hand in his hair one last time. Breathed her in one last time.

When he stood and found his mother again,

her expression was tortured. He knew how she felt about bringing young into the clan.

"Thomas, what have you done?"

"We," Marlee interrupted. "What have *we* done."

His mother looked between the two of them, her face running a gamut of emotions.

"Are you with young?" she breathed.

Marlee frowned. Looked to Ratchet.

"Yes, ma. She's carrying my cub."

His mother seemed to age ten years right before his eyes.

"But I'm doing it right. I'm getting them both out of here. Far away from this life. They're going to be safe, away from me. Away from the crew. Away from the hate and the curse and all of it. Mom, I'm not letting mine be hurt. See? I'm doing right by them."

She blinked over and over. Seconds passed. He couldn't guess what was going through her mind, but eventually she nodded. "We... we need to go then. Right now. Before it's too late."

Marlee moved for the door, but his mother stopped her. "No! Uh, let's take the roof."

Ratchet frowned.

"Changed my mind. Don't want to chance taking her through the offices. I think it will be safer to cross the roof and go down the other fire escape. The one by the shed. No one ever goes over there."

"Okay." He pulled Marlee toward the window, climbing out first and helping his mom onto the landing.

He reached back in for Marlee, but she was over at the dresser writing something on a piece of paper.

Scanning the lot, he motioned for his mother to start climbing, and looked back in to see Marlee messing with the bed pillows before she ran to the window carrying her loaded down duffle bag.

He helped her out, and stood watch as she climbed up after his mom.

And then they were all on the roof, and his beast rumbled inside feeling all the mixed up pain and satisfaction. Pain of losing something so precious. Satisfaction knowing he was doing the best thing for the people he loved.

Loved. Fuck yeah.

He'd done it.

Whether it broke the curse or not, he'd learned to love. And love hard. He couldn't love his Marlee any harder. And if that wasn't enough to undo what the witches did to him, then fuck it. Because he'd made magic of his own. And it was growing inside his mate.

And best of all? He could do the noble damn thing. He could do it even though it hurt like hell. And nothing felt righter than doing the noble damn thing *for her*.

The lion could protect the lamb.

It just meant... he had to sacrifice.

Well... done. Fucking. Deal.

"No time to waste," his mother murmured.

Ratchet turned to Marlee. Shit. This was it.

He pulled her close, dropping the softest kiss to her lips. But he hadn't even finished when a sob escaped her throat and she pressed in hard enough their teeth clashed. He tasted her tears, her breath, and soaked it all in to keep for later.

Staring into her emerald eyes, he told her the truth…

"You're Marlee Benson," he whispered. "You're twenty-eight years old. And you are finally free. I love you. Don't forget, don't forget, don't forget."

Tears streamed down her cheeks and he didn't bother wiping them away.

His mother wrapped an arm around Marlee's shoulder and led her across the roof.

His heart attacked his ribs as he watched her walk away, fighting back the tears that wanted free of his eyes. And while the mangled thing was breaking, pieces of it shattering and raining down like broken glass, all he could think was… he was so damn proud of her.

So fucking proud of his mate. His mate that carried his baby. His mate that he'd never see again. Because that's what it took to make her safe. And he would always, *always* choose the thing that kept her safe.

It was a promise he'd take to his grave.

Twenty

Brokenhearted, Marlee followed Leah down the ladder on the other side of the roof. The one that didn't come out near Felix's window. The one that would lead her to the shed. To the place where it all began.

She dashed her tears away. They wouldn't quit coming, but she hefted the duffle onto her shoulder and tried to be brave like Ratchet believed she could be.

Jumping from the ladder to the lot, she landed with a quiet thud and followed Leah to the long metal building where she'd taken shelter after escaping Bastian.

Everything had come full circle.

Her captor was her liberator. Her despair was her hope. Her escape was the place she'd been snared.

It was irony, or she had the worst luck of any human alive.

But this part of her story wasn't over. No matter what Ratchet said, this was not goodbye.

It was only goodbye *for now*.

"Come on, hun," Leah rushed. "We need to get you in the shed before anyone sees. Once you're in, you move straight for those back doors. It's dark in there. Watch for the empty barrels. The door on the left will open to the street. You wait out there in the alley, and I'll bring the truck around. We'll get you to the station and on a bus and..." The older lady sighed, looking down at Marlee's stomach, and her face broke into the saddest smile. "You take care of that baby, okay? Tell him about his grandma Leah. That you didn't get to know her that well, but she made good chocolate cake and bad choices. But it all worked out in the end."

Marlee nodded, more tears coming. She pushed her chin forward. "I will. I promise."

With a big breath, Leah pulled open the door to the shed.

But before Marlee could slip inside, the area flooded with light and an earsplitting alarm went off.

She froze. Leah did too, looking confused and panicked.

Boots crunching on the gravel as someone neared couldn't even spur them into moving. The alarm was loud enough to wake the entire block. The kind that announced a fire or... or... *something*.

A tall, wide man covered in brightly colored tattoos skidded to a halt in front of them.

"Aw shit, Mama. What are you doing?" His eyes were big and round as they went from Leah to Marlee and back. "I told you to stay away from the shed."

Marlee recognized the voice. This was either Skittles or Monster. Going off the tattoos and lack of facial scars, she was going to guess Skittles.

"I-I-I changed my mind," Leah stuttered. "I couldn't do it. She's with young."

Skittles' eyes went impossibly wider as his gaze fell to Marlee's abdomen.

She stared at Leah who'd turned pale. Couldn't do what?

"Hell, Mama," Skittles spat. "I wasn't going to hurt her. I was going to ask for her help."

Help doing what?

But she couldn't ask because the sound of more people running toward them had her panic soaring. A low, eerie whistle floated along the air as men came to a stop behind Skittles. Some stumbling like they were drunk, but snarling like they were ready to fight. Others, lucid, glaring angrily. They crowded around her and Leah, seemingly awaiting a command.

Alley Cats. So many of them. Enough she

knew she wasn't getting out of there unharmed.

Skittles caught her gaze, staring hard. He was trying to tell her something, but she couldn't know what.

The sing-song whistle grew louder as one last set of footsteps strolled closer. This one was leisurely, as if he was enjoying making them all wait. And when he finally pushed through the crowd, revealing a huge shell of a man who must have at one time been strong and fierce, she knew she was looking at Felix.

He carried that familiar Alley Cat snarl and his golden eyes seemed morbidly excited. Like a predator who was anxious to give chase. A different kind of lion... who'd found a lamb.

"Well, well, well," he purred, pacing closer. His voice sent chills of terror rolling over Marlee's skin. *Dangerous.* This one was dangerous. And not like Ratchet was. Felix would hurt her. Hurt anyone. "What *the fuck* do we have here, cats?"

"Mama Kitty found her getting in the shed," Skittles lied easily. He grabbed Marlee roughly by the arm, earning a cry. She clamped her mouth shut, remembering Ratchet's warning. *Don't look weak.* "I'll get rid of her."

"Not so fast," Felix said, narrowing his gaze on her. "She's new. And pretty. And she cries. Maybe I want to play with her."

"No," Leah said, her voice snapping out like a whip. "You don't need to do that, okay? You have women upstairs who want you. Use them."

His expression went hard and he twisted his gaze to Ratchet's mother. "Since when do you care who I play with, Mama Kitty? Huh?"

He marched forward, ripping Marlee's arm from Skittles' grasp and twisting it behind her back. She hissed at his nearness, but his hands were less rough than Skittles'. He was weaker, even if he was meaner.

"What's this female to you, Mama?"

Felix stared down into her face turning her toward the light so he could get a good look. And Marlee saw when recognition dawned in his eyes.

"I know you," he growled. "You're Bastian's.

He's been looking for you, little girl."

The words did something to her. Hit her all wrong. Brought her fight back a hundredfold.

"Not *his*," she snarled back at him. "Never his. I belong to the one who gives more than he gets. The one who *set me free*." She jerked her arm in his hold, not caring about the pain it brought.

Felix tightened his grip, growling out an earsplitting warning. But she didn't care. She wasn't giving up without a fight. And she wasn't letting him take her back to Bastian.

Being free meant she was never going back.

A crackle of energy whipped through the air, jerking everyone to attention. Even Felix. It was like static electricity making the small hairs on her arm stand on end.

"Get. Your. Hands off her." The voice was deadly, and almost unrecognizable. But she would recognize her man anywhere. And he sounded so damn good right about now.

"Ratchet?" Felix sounded confused. But when Ratchet stepped into the light, glowing eyes narrowed on Marlee, furious scowl leveled on the place where Felix had her arm twisted, the Alley Cat leader seemed to laugh him off. "Shit, man. What happened to you? You look like hell."

"Take your hands off my woman. *Now.*" The last word ended on a threatening growl as the crowd parted for him and he stalked forward looking for all the world like a warrior intent on leaving a trail of blood behind him.

Animal, she thought.

"Your woman?" Felix scoffed looking more shocked than he probably meant to. "Since when do you have a woman, Ratchet? You steal her from Bastian? Because if you did, I don't think I can help you. He wants her dead. You fucked up, man."

Ratchet shook with fury and Felix dropped her arm, throwing his hands up.

"Fine. Shit. I'll be taking this out of your skin, asshole," he seethed, eyes narrowed.

Marlee noticed Leah balk. Felix was going to cut him for this.

"No one. Touches. Her. No one touches *mine.*"

The other Alley Cats shifted nervously, looking back and forth between their leader and Ratchet.

Felix gave him a ruthless smirk. "She won't be yours for long. I'm giving her back to Bastian. Along with your mother as a peace offering." He shot Leah a cruel look. "Sorry, Mama, really. But you shouldn't have betrayed your clan like this. Now I have to fix this shit."

"Wait," Skittles said. "We giving Bastian our own? We doing *that* now?"

"Fuck yeah," Felix snapped. "You rather die, asshole?"

Skittles didn't answer. Felix spun to face the others.

"We die at Bastian's hand if he finds out we have his property and didn't give it back. Weak fuckers, all of you. Maybe it's time for another *flaying*. Remind you all what *the fuck* you really are."

Ratchet growled, stepping between Marlee and his leader. She felt the heat rolling off of him, warming the cool night air. So much heat. She wanted to reach out and touch him one more time. But he vibrated with so much emotion it seemed he would break apart.

"She's going back. Right now. That's a motherfucking order. Monster, Fang. Grab her. Mama Kitty will go willingly. Won't you, Mama?"

"Ratchet?" Marlee whimpered.

His fists clenched. Open and shut. Again and again.

And she must have been panic-hallucinating because it looked like they were sparking.

He turned to find her over his shoulder. And his eyes flared that fiery blue. But more. There were... there were... *flames.*

"Run, lamb."

It was the last words he said to her before his body exploded into a ripping, snarling, avenging ball of fire.

Twenty One

We burn. We burn free.

Ratchet glared at Felix. At Skittles and Monster. At his entire clan.

We burn. We burn free.

They wouldn't be hurting anyone tonight.

We burn. We burn free.

The beast inside chanted the phrase, directing Ratchet's fury to the heart of him and letting it fuel something brand new. Something amazing. Something that was going to change *everything*.

Because he knew the truth now.

He *was* enough for Marlee. He'd only needed to believe it.

Letting her go had finished the curse. The ultimate sacrifice. One done in love. True, unconditional, unselfish love. It was the key.

It was the cure.

For so much more than just the curse. It was the thing that would save them all.

Starting with his mate.

He was enough. He would be her protector for the rest of his days and show his clan the way. Show them how to be human enough to deserve a shifter.

The most powerful shifter of all.

Pain like he'd never endured shot through his limbs. Pure fire hotter than any hell flame, reminding him of his past transgressions. Reminding him this was his new beginning and payment for the sins he'd committed all rolled into one burning purification.

This was his redemption.

The firecat ripped Ratchet's body to pieces as it roared to a victorious shift. Human skin became rippling lion's fur. Fisting fingers became deadly razored claws. His golden hair became a mane of fire, flickering around his head, roaring in his ears as it burned. So hot.

But not consuming.

He let off a vicious roar, twisting his massive head in every direction. A declaration to the world.

I am a King of beasts. And my Queen will not be harmed.

"Fuck." Felix cowered backward, too close to the burst of fire Ratchet spewed from his throat. He smelled the sharp scent of singed hair from his leader's arms.

It was a warning.

The next time, he wouldn't miss.

Felix's hands went up, feigning surrender. "How?" he asked. "Tell me how you broke the damn curse."

Ratchet paced a boundary in front of the Alley

Cats, letting his flaming body lick heat at them as he made pass after pass.

Look on me. Never cross me.

"Son of a bitch," Felix snarled. "Tell me how you did this."

Ratchet let off another roar.

"*He* didn't," Skittles spoke up. "The female did."

Felix glared at his second. "Explain."

Skittles pulled the photo from his vest pocket and held it up for all to see.

Monster let off a warning growl but Skittles ignored him.

"These are Bastian's dolls. Like this one, we have to free them. They are the answer to healing our beasts. Or... some of them at least. One is mine. She calls to my beast. Whatever happened to Malcom, Ratchet... it can happen for all of us. But we have to change. That's what the Sorcera said. The curse only breaks with a change." He turned to Felix. "You want to know how? His girl made him *feel*. Changed him. Like the fathers did

320

with us, except pure. She made him fear something bigger than… you. Bigger than this clan."

Felix shook his head, glaring, but Ratchet saw the wheels turning behind his eyes. The hunger for power. The desire to be strong again. Feared again.

"Fear what?"

Skittles stared at the photo. Squinted hard. Swallowed until his throat bobbed.

"Life without *her*," he muttered.

He shook his head, looking uneasy and stuffed the picture back in his vest. Edging forward, he drew near to Ratchet, head bowed in deference to the beast. When he was close enough that the heat from the firecat could burn him, he dropped to his knees on the gravel… and bowed.

Ratchet growled warily, smoke chuffing from his nostrils as he stared at his brother.

What was this?

"I want to fight for the future," Skittles rumbled. "This is the way. I pledge to you."

One by one, Alley Cats took to their knees, following Skittles' lead. Half of them were drunk, but you couldn't tell it from their sobered expressions. Hopeful even. Plenty would want the firecat for the wrong reasons. But the best part of the curse was that they couldn't get it unless it was for the right ones.

A failsafe that had almost cost him his future. He was so glad he chose right. Chose freedom.

Ratchet needed to thank the Sorcera someday. With or without the curse, he might've found Marlee. But without it, he wouldn't have become the man she needed.

The fire of the beast faded as he stared at his brothers. They wanted him to lead them out of the darkness. But it wasn't his job.

He found Felix desperately trying to hide the devastation of seeing his clan bow before another. One more powerful than him.

Ratchet shifted, letting his new animal fall away until he was human again. Skin and bone reforming, and he stood, taking in his brothers.

The raw feelings rushing at him as they struggled to make sense of all that was happening.

"I'm not your leader," he bellowed. "Felix is. He put you here. He's your fucking Moses. I'm only here to make sure he does right by you. Understand?" Ratchet turned to the broken man with the broken beast. With his crippled, fucked up heart that maybe could never be redeemed. "You lead your people. Do it fucking right. And we will *all* follow."

Felix stared him down, jaw tight. Stared for so long Ratchet wondered if they would battle. He didn't want to put Felix down. He knew the man had been formed with cruel and vicious hands like they all had. But if Ratchet could change... if Skittles could, or Monster... then there was still hope for the cruelest of them all.

The savage heart.

Felix nodded slowly. His eyes went dull and he stared across the lot at his people before turning back to Ratchet.

"Fine. You want war with Bastian? You better

be prepared for the fallout."

With that, he stalked off toward the warehouse.

Little by little the cats scattered until only Skittles, Monster, and Fang remained. They got to their feet, none of them looking unshaken.

Fang eyed Ratchet. He still had his beer in his hand and his fly was down. "So, uh... cool trick, bro."

"Shut up, asshole."

Fang shrugged. "What? Just saying."

Ratchet turned to find Marlee, but she was nowhere to be seen. His mother stood in the door of the shed, tears rolling down her cheeks.

"Where is she?" he asked.

But she shook her head sadly. "She left. You said run, Thomas. She did."

Wait. Marlee was gone?

His breath stalled imagining what she must have thought when his beast came out. Shit, she probably thought he was a monster. But the monster was who he used to be. The thing he was now could protect her. Would guard her like the most precious treasure.

He could finally keep her safe and now she was running from him.

Fuck.

He had to find her.

Hunt mate. Track her scent.

Ratchet's lips twisted in a satisfied smirk. He could do that now.

"Spread out. Find her. But don't fucking scare her." He gave Fang a warning glare. "I need your pants."

It wasn't a good idea, wearing Fang's pants... shit, nasty bastard... but he couldn't go looking for his mate buck-ass naked.

"Excuse me, what?"

"Your pants. Give me your fucking pants."

Fang laughed. "Not happening. These are mine. Go find your own drawers."

"Hand 'em over or I take your nuts."

"What would you do with them though? That's the question."

Ratchet let off a smoky growl and Fang jumped back.

"Okay, okay. Barbecued nuts don't sound like my kind-a fun." He dropped his jeans, hopping on one foot to get them past his boot. But he was too wasted and ended up on his ass while seconds ticked off and Marlee got farther away.

Ratchet sent Skittles and Monster ahead, following when he was finally in Fang's nasty jeans. He left his mother to deal with the cat.

He had a mate to catch.

He ran, barefoot across the lot, letting his new beast be his guide, feeling the freedom of being whole. He'd never take his power... *his gift*... for granted again.

Mate is close, the beast purred.

He'd follow her scent like a fucking bloodhound until he found her and kissed her silly. He'd explain his firecat. Show her he was safe. Like he had before. With gifts and soft touches and patience.

Then he was keeping her.

Forever.

*****

Marlee paced the darkness of her small hiding spot with only the flashlight to keep her steady, trying to make sense of what she'd just witnessed.

A burning lion.

Her man was a burning lion.

Okay.

No. Not okay.

What the hell.

Ratchet told her he had an animal inside him. He'd warned her. But couldn't he have done more? Like... like...

She sighed.

Right. How did you put a warning label on that?

She recalled what he'd said to Skittles and Monster when she was hiding in the bathroom. *To heal our animals, break the curse the witches put on us, we have to change in our hearts.*

327

It had all seemed so symbolic. She thought they were talking their clan speak.

Or when Ratchet sensed she was pregnant. *My animal, it's in me, and it knew.*

Which made her wonder...

She pressed a shaking palm to her belly. Was this baby a burning lion too?

Or when he set her free because he had no way to keep her safe. *I wasn't enough. I can't bring the firecat out, no matter how much I love you. I can't protect you.*

But now he could. He had.

Ratchet stood up to his clan, to Felix. And he would do the same against Bastian.

This meant she could stay. It meant they could be a family. That she didn't have to do things alone.

It meant...

It meant she'd be living with a beast. And while that worked out for Belle, this wasn't a fairytale. This was somehow real life.

Ratchet was a burning lion. And she was a

lamb.

Did she trust him enough to swallow all this down like it was nothing? To be with him in this strange existence. To fight for the dolls with him and the others.

For the first time in a long time, she had a choice.

What will you do, Marlee?

She gripped the flashlight to her chest as she paced in the dark. The dark she so hated.

She stared at the light. It was one of those hard metal ones that was bright as day. It lit up her entire hiding spot.

Ratchet packed it for her. So she'd have it for a time just like this. In case she was forced into the darkness.

He'd done that. Thought of her fears and made a way to battle them back.

The breath eased out of her chest as she realized... he always would.

Because that's *who* he was. *What* he was didn't matter.

Treasures from the trash. "Glitter" Girls and chocolate cake. Holding pinkies and taking her *no* as law. That was the Ratchet she knew and loved. The one who cared so much about her safety he'd set her free. If he happened to have a burning beast in him, then yeah, fine. She loved a beast.

And now she was using her freedom to return to him.

Twenty Two

Ratchet slammed his bedroom door in frustration. He couldn't find his lamb. She was nowhere. They'd searched the property and followed her trail out to the alley. Where it disappeared at the street. Now the guys were driving around the area looking—with the warning that Ratchet would fry anyone who touched her.

But it was pointless, he knew.

She was gone. Fucking gone.

He shucked Fang's pants and tossed them in

the basket. Then he thought better of it, and threw them in the garbage.

Stalking to the bathroom, he gave the shower faucet an angry twist and stepped under the spray, not waiting for the water to warm up. The cold wouldn't bother him now.

His mom had come clean about her plan to have Skittles take Marlee back to Bastian. And Skittles had told him he'd only considered it because he hoped she would tell him the name of his girl. And maybe help him find a way to get her free.

But his mom had a change of heart and took Marlee out through the shed where Felix and Skittles had put a fucking alarm.

Ratchet's suggestion, Skittles reminded him.

No matter what their intentions were, the idea that he'd almost given Marlee to the wolf-in-sheep's clothing sat all wrong with him.

He wouldn't make that mistake again. His beast would guide his instincts. And he'd trust no one with his mate's safety.

If he ever found her.

He cranked off the water and stepped out of the shower, snapping a towel free and wrapping it around his waist.

In the room, he stood staring at the bed. He didn't want to get in it. Not ever.

He'd take the chair. The fucking chair.

But he wasn't sleeping anyway. He just needed to think. About Marlee and where she might go. And come morning, he was going after her. Maybe she didn't want to see him, but he had to explain things.

He pulled on his own jeans, not spending the effort to button them, and grabbed a beer from the fridge, popping it open and gulping half of it down in one swig. He put his ass in the chair and reached for her pillow, bringing it to his nose to breathe her sweet scent. It was a thousand times stronger now with his sharper senses.

Oh, shit. He missed her so much already. He drew in a trembling breath and brushed away the fucking wetness from his eyes.

His beast whimpered inside, pacing and demanding he do *something*.

"Like what?" he growled.

He gripped the pillow in his fist, hard enough to rip the fabric. But he didn't want to ruin it. He needed as much of her scent as possible to keep him sane until he found her. Instead, he threw it against the wall.

Ratchet frowned as a slip of paper fluttered free of the pillowcase and landed on the floor.

The hell?

Pushing to a stand and setting his beer on the floor, he walked over, bending to retrieve it. In rushed scribble, were the words:

I'm coming back for the marble. In the meantime, look for me in the stars. I'll be the one holding your pinky.

Ratchet blinked, reading Marlee's message again.

She'd planned on coming back. Maybe not right away, but she had wanted to battle her way back to him when he'd made it safe for her. She hadn't realized without the firecat, it never would've been safe enough.

And now that it was...

He stood, unable to take his eyes off her message.

Shit.

His beast chuffed at the pain lighting up his chest.

He swiped at his tears again. He was really crying. Fuck, whatever. This was who he was now. Half a man without her.

He'd been missing a piece of himself for so long. But the beast didn't make him whole. Marlee had.

Look for me in the stars.

Feeling lost and wanting to remember, he ducked out his window and climbed the ladder to the roof, doubling back for his beer.

In the open air of the rooftop, he paced out his sadness, her note hanging limply from his fingers, the bottle of beer staying mostly at his lips.

He didn't bother with the tears now. He just

wanted to focus on being here where they watched the stars so many nights. Where he touched her for the first time. He could still remember the fluttering in his chest when she pressed her little pinky to his, waiting to see what he'd do. He'd taken a chance. It felt like the biggest fucking risk at the time. But he'd curled his finger around hers.

And she didn't pull away.

And he knew he was lost to her right then. Completely fucking lost.

"Shit." The curse left his mouth sounding soaked. And he still didn't care. "Shit, shit."

He downed the rest of his beer and flung the bottle at the door of the utility room where it crashed against the metal, splintering into a million pieces.

A high-pitched yelp from behind the door had him going ramrod stiff.

"Marlee?"

He crossed the roof to the utility room, yanking open the door and damn near pulling it off the hinges.

Damn it. He'd have to be careful with this strength.

Another surprised gasp caught his attention as the light from outside flooded into the room. He found her standing in the middle of the small space, flashlight in hand, blinking against the brightness.

"Marlee," he breathed.

"Ratchet," she cried, and rushed him, dropping her flashlight as her arms came around his waist and her face burrowed into his bare chest.

Shaking all to hell, he cradled her head, swallowing over and over to keep his emotion behind his fucking throat.

"I'm staying," she said. "You have the cat now... whatever the hell it is... so I'm staying. Me and little firekitten. Don't even try to stop me, Ratchet, because I'm staying. I'm staying, okay. There's nowhere else I should be. I'm stayi—"

He brought her face up, forgetting to be

gentle, because she was here, and all he wanted to do was taste her again. Get her under his body so he could claim her the right way. Fuck away all the shit they'd been through tonight. Get her back in his bed where he could hold her while they slept.

He pressed his lips to hers, tasting their tears as his tongue plowed inside, desperately needing to claim every inch of her mouth.

She clung to him, her short nails scraping into the skin of his back as she hungrily met his tongue thrust for thrust.

He broke away, holding her face close. Didn't want any space between them.

"Been looking everywhere for you, lamb." As he whispered, his lips brushed hers.

"I was right here," she whispered back.

"Were you scared? Of me?"

"No," she said, shaking her head where his was pressed to hers. "Surprised. Confused. Still am a little. But you turned back into... *you*. And I trust you. Ratchet, I *trust* you."

He heard what she was saying. Heard it deep

in his heart. In their bond. In the part of him she controlled, and always would.

But she whispered it anyway. "I love you."

Aw, shit. That was all he needed to hear. All the pieces of his broken heart were locking back into place like a fucking miracle.

His beast rumbled his chest in approval.

He crushed his lips to hers hard enough to bruise.

Shit, careful.

But she kissed him back, and her fingers tangled in his hair pulling hard enough to bring his cock roaring to life. Desperate Marlee was a new thing, and he liked her like this.

He cut the kiss short, hooking her pinky and dragging her out of the utility room.

"Wait. Where are we going?"

"To bed."

"The duffle," she said, but they were already halfway across the roof.

"Leave it. I need inside you," he growled.

"Okay. Okay good. Yeah."

He skipped most of the steps on the ladder, jumping to the bottom instead and waiting for her to make her way down.

"Careful, lamb."

When she was two steps from the bottom, he was done waiting. He lifted her off the ladder and carried her to his window, setting her safely inside before climbing through himself.

"I'll try not to scare you," he murmured, stalking toward her where she stood just beside the bed. "Try my best. But I thought I lost you, lamb."

"You can't scare me." Her breath churned, making her small breasts heave. "Not like this. Not with you. You're my safe place. My protector. My warrior."

Mmmm. Yessss. He was that.

"Take off your shirt," he rasped. Because he couldn't. If he got any closer, he was going to rip it off. Tear it to shreds with his claws.

Marlee peeled it over her head, letting it land on the floor.

340

"Now your bra." That sexy scrap of lacy fabric she'd ordered online... it made him hard as steel, but it had to go. He wanted her bare to him for what was coming.

She shrugged it off, leaving just her perfect tits with their hard pink tips and her jeans.

"The rest," he croaked, and she hurried to get her pants down, kicking them away. He freed himself of his too, and then there was nothing else between them except air.

Ratchet breathed deep, scenting his mate's arousal. It brought a purr from his beast, and Marlee's eyes flared when she heard it.

"Your animal." She didn't cower. She only seemed... curious.

"The beast won't hurt you. He's safe. Not like my old animal. Not like the Alley Cat I was born with. This one's part of me and he only exists because of you."

"I'm not scared."

"Good." Ratchet stepped closer. He was going to take her down to the bed in the next breath or two. "Because he wants to claim you for his mate. Wants to make you *mine*. It means forever."

"He does. Or you do?"

"Both."

"Good."

And his control snapped.

He lunged for his mate, taking her to the bed and breaking her fall with his arms.

"Oh, lamb," he rasped against her throat. "I'm going to eat. You. Up."

***

Marlee moaned at the feel of Ratchet's hard body pressing her into the mattress. His lips were doing wicked things to her neck. His hands were trying to touch every part of her at once.

Wild.

He was always careful with her. Soft touches. And she loved those. Did she ever. They'd brought her back from the ugliest time of her life and made her feel human again. Made her feel special and cared for.

Those soft touches coming from a hard man

had saved her life.

But he wasn't careful now. He was wild. He was showing her the rest of him.

And she loved this side even more.

She could make him lose control, she realized. She could make her powerful man lose all control, and for once, she... she didn't want him to be careful. She wanted him to be raw and feral. An animal.

She should probably want answers to all of her firecat questions. But all she could think about was being one with him again. Connecting in that way that she felt deep in her middle. Like they breathed the same air, pumped the same blood.

Questions could come later. And she had a lot for him.

Right now, she wanted to make him lose all sense. Lose control. Wanted him as out of his mind as she was.

So she bit him.

Just a small bite. On the chord of muscle above his shoulder. It was a sexy spot. Teeth seemed like a good idea.

Call it instinct, call it risky. Either way, it resulted in the desired effect.

Ratchet went still, his chest pumping with that sexy purr. He found her gaze, staring at her with those flaming blue eyes, tinged orange with the evidence of his cat.

"Did you just *bite* me, lamb." He stared through the hair that hung in his face, the familiar snarl she loved twisting his lips.

She nodded, pressing her lips together to keep from moaning at the way he looked at her.

He dove for her mouth, prying open her lips with his tongue and then leisurely sucking the lower one into his mouth and letting it pop free before nibbling his way back down her neck.

His needy hand probed lower and lower until he cupped her sex. Her legs fell open for him this time, knowing he was never going to go too far. Never going to hurt her. Only make her squirm. Only make her float high.

He rubbed her with the heel of his hand, his

finger dipping in to test her wetness. But she was ready. So close to release and he wasn't even in her yet.

He must have come to the same conclusion, because he lined up at her entrance, pressing in with one smooth stroke.

Marlee gasped at the sensation. The drag of his body pushing into hers was something she would never get enough of.

He went still when he was buried deep, panting with restraint.

"I want to take you hard. Make you feel me hard. But I won't, lamb. I'll be careful with you. Always."

His eyes went soft with his promise, and she melted beneath him. Always thinking of her. Always giving more than he got.

True love. The purest love.

She vowed to love him back the very same way.

Ratchet pulled back and plunged forward, pushing into her easy, determined to keep his promise. He moved again, watching her face while he made love to her.

"Harder," she groaned. "Like you want to. Do it. I want it."

But instead, he slowed, staring hard at her. Brow furrowed tight, eyes blazing, he warned, "You don't know what you're saying."

"Yes, I do. I want you wild. Do what you said you'd do. Make me yours."

He didn't move. He only stared, mouth open to resist.

But she wasn't letting him.

She leaned up, nipping his jaw with her teeth and earning a low snarl. He pulled back and this time plunged forward hard enough to rock her entire body and the bed with it.

She cried out in pleasure, groaning for more.

"Hard, lamb?" His voice was deceptively soft. The opposite of his body. "You want me to take you hard."

Another body shaking thrust, and another.

"On one condition..." He sucked in a sharp

breath when she clenched around him, just a breath away from a mind-shattering orgasm.

"Anything," she squealed, as he bottomed out again, vibrating her teeth.

"You promise me forever. I want it, lamb."

Thrust.

"You."

Thrust.

"Me."

Thrust.

"And firekitten. Say yes."

Forever with a man who put her first? Who cared about her safety, her future, her wants and needs. Who was strong enough to battle all her demons. The ones in her mind and the ones in life.

That was the easiest yes of her existence.

"Yes."

With her whispered vow, the hold on his restraint snapped, and Ratchet became a snarling, lust-crazed beast, driving into her, over and over. He pushed her up the bed with each thrust, spread her legs wider to get deeper. His hair hung over his sweat slicked face, and his eyes never left hers as he pistoned into her.

She could have come from his look alone. The pure ownership there. The way his eyes screamed *you're mine.*

But it was the feel of his hand on her hip that sent her over the edge. The way he gripped her as he pounded her. Soft. The soft touch in the storm of lust. It reminded her he could always be soft for her. He could be hard for her. He could be whatever she needed.

She screamed as pleasure rattled her from head to toe, making her jerk and spasm around Ratchet.

He threw his head back roaring his approval and filling her with his hot release.

A sharp pain at her hip was barely a blip on her radar as her body went into another fit, writhing and clamping and gasping, like she was possessed. But she had no shame. It felt too good, and there was something else.

The bond. The feeling in her middle that

made her want to cling to him. Something was happening to it.

It was growing stronger. Becoming solid. It felt... unbreakable.

Ratchet gave one last hard push into her body and then collapsed on top of her, breathing hard.

She clamped her mouth shut when she realized she was making whale noises. Or goat grunts. It was something hideous anyway. What the hell?

But he'd just broken her with sex. Broken her in the best way, and put her back together.

He was good at that. Taking things that were trashed and making treasures out of them.

Ratchet pulled up, angling his face toward her hip. Cold air hit her and she felt something wet. Somehow she lifted her head to find him blowing on her skin. A tiny trail of blood trickled from a jagged claw mark and he dabbed at it with the sheet.

She frowned. "What is it?"

It didn't hurt. Did he get a little too wild?

Because she wasn't holding it against him—

"I marked you," he said quietly. "A mating mark. To let the world know. You're marked with my scent too."

"I am?"

He nodded, glancing at her and looking so satisfied she wanted to kiss the look off his face.

"Humans won't notice, but other shifters will, and they won't dare touch you."

"Shifter. Is that what you are? What firekitten will be?"

He nodded, rolling to the side and pulling her into his arms.

"I was a werecat. We all were. Skittles, Monster, Fang... Felix. The others."

"Your mom?"

He stiffened. "No, she's human. I got the cat from my father."

"Oh." She nuzzled his chest so he'd keep going.

"But we did a bad thing and made the wrong people angry. We threatened innocents." He swallowed hard. "Not fucking proud of it, lamb. But it's how the story goes. To stop us, a coven of witches called Sorcera put a curse on us that crippled our animals. Locked them inside our bodies where they faded away to nothing. The only way to break the curse is to have a change of heart."

"Fall in love," she whispered.

Ratchet nodded. "But more than that. I loved you, and still couldn't pull the firecat free. It took something more. It took sacrifice. A selfless action. Something pure enough to burn it all away. All the dark past and shit."

"Setting me free," she realized. "To keep me and firekitten safe, you let us go."

And the curse was broken.

He squeezed her close, dropping kisses to her hair.

"It's over now. We're both fixed, you and me," he murmured. "Things won't always be easy for us, lamb. But I won't ever let you face shit alone. I swear it."

Across the sheet, she found his pinky. She curled hers around it in a silent promise to always meet him in the darkness, even if it scared the hell out of her.

"What now?" she asked.

Ratchet squeezed her finger. "I like when you ask me that."

She shivered and he pulled the sheet over them, making sure she was covered to her chin.

"Now we make a plan to get the dolls free. We hope like hell some of these fuckers can do what it takes to break the curse. And then..." His voice went dark. "...we take Bastian down. And make Memphis a shit-bit safer."

It sounded like a good plan. Perfect even. Except for one thing.

"And live happily ever after?"

Ratchet smirked. "And maybe some of that, lamb."

He brought her pinky to his lips and kissed the promise there before doing it again on her mouth.

And she knew they'd be all right. All of them. The clan. The dolls. The future.

Because she had a man who was good at making people safe.

And he could breathe fire. So.

Epilogue

Three weeks later...

Monster waited on the landing of Bastian Marx's fancypants billion-dollar home. The thing looked like it was paid for with deceit and trickery and smelled like the tears of the defeated.

Or maybe that was just because he knew what was inside.

Four girls that didn't deserve to be locked in a cold fucking basement while they paid off whatever debt they or somebody else owed.

But he hadn't had to fight to get past the

security at the front gate. No, he'd walked right through because they were expecting him. And as the door opened, he was greeted by a smiling maid in a black and white dress. Creepy as fuck. It was like a movie he'd seen recently.

"You must be here for the security position, yes?"

Monster nodded and the female smiled pleasantly, even though she was having a hard time looking at his scars. He couldn't blame her. They were ugly ass things. And right there on his face. Like a billboard announcing he was ugly inside too.

But not for long, the voice inside whispered. That new amazing voice that gave him fucking hope. *Find her, and she will help you.*

But he was here for a slow gig. To gain entry to Bastian's home. Gain his trust. Get close to the dolls, so he and the other Alley Cats could get them free.

The female led him through a maze of hallways to a set of double doors. He logged the path in his mind as she knocked and announced him.

Shit, Bastian liked life fancy, didn't he?

Maybe this was good news. Maybe his girl wasn't living in such bad conditions as his mind had imagined. Marlee had told him of a basement. Said it was dark and cold. Just cement and a few beds that had to be shared. And never enough blankets.

Monster swallowed hard.

He hated the idea of his girl being cold.

Shivering on the floor. Huddled in for warmth she wouldn't find. He pictured her, the way she was in the photo, and he couldn't imagine her any other way but cold.

Find her, and take her. Come back later for the others.

But Monster knew it would only get the dolls hurt. If he even made it out of the mansion with his. It would put their entire plan in jeopardy, and he'd promised Marlee he wouldn't risk *any* of the girls.

The maid pulled the doors wide, ushering Monster into an office that looked grander than the fucking president's. Bastian, the fucking excessive bastard, sat in a plush leather chair, puffing slowly on a cigar. His slightly balding head didn't so much as shift as he regarded Monster with disdain.

"Why you here?" he asked, his northeastern accent coming through to make 'here' sound like heeyeh. "I ordered a Junkyard Dog. Not a filthy Alley Cat."

"They were out of stock," Monster said lazily. "Besides, you get me for free since Felix couldn't find your missing girl. Take it or leave it. I'd rather be drinking Jack and fucking anyway."

Not true. He hadn't thought of fucking in so long, he wondered if he'd even remember how to. And he'd consumed a lot less whiskey since seeing his girl's picture. He couldn't remember her face when he was drunk, so he'd been staying a lot more sober.

Bastian narrowed his good eye and put his

cigar out in the crystal ashtray. Who the fuck used a crystal ashtray? A man who thought he was king, that's who. A fucking lord of Memphis.

"This one is a special assignment. Requires steel for balls. Can't be soft, not even a little. You up for that?"

"My face should tell you I'm far from soft."

Scars like his came from being fucked up a lot. Which would make anyone hard as steel.

Bastian sighed, using his cane to stand. He was a tall man. A few inches taller than Monster's 6'3". But his bad leg and the way he limped made him seem less.

He came around the desk, staring at Monster like he was trying to read him, and then he nodded, satisfied.

"You'll do," he murmured. "You'll do just fine. A face like that is exactly what I need to scare my dolls into obedience. Follow me."

He led Monster down a staircase and another maze of halls before reaching a plain white door in the wall. It wasn't hidden exactly, but it looked like it was supposed to seem unimportant. Especially compare to the other doors in the house with their ornate molding and sculpted handles.

Monster followed Bastian through and into a dark hallway. This one wasn't brightly lit. There was a small lamp in the corner, and nothing else as they maneuvered a steep thin staircase.

"I have two rules. You break these rules, and I break you. For good, understand? These are my dolls and I don't take chances with them."

Monster grit his teeth as the air grew colder.

"No touching the dolls. That's number one. I have cameras on them now. Since Thirteen escaped. I see you touch one, you're dead. Easy like that."

"Understood."

Another dim lamp lit the bottom of the stairs, and it was exactly as Marlee described. Dark. Cold. Hopeless.

Monster's stomach churned. His girl was down here. He was going to see her, face to face.

How was he going to keep from stealing her away to safety?

Shit, he'd promised Marlee something he didn't know if he could keep.

"And rule number two…"

Bastian stopped outside a new door. This one plain like the first, but containing several heavy duty locks, including an electronic one. He tapped out a sequence on the keypad and pulled a chain of keys from his pocket for the rest before turning back to Monster.

"Scare the hell outta them," he snarled. "I want them pissing their pants when they see you. Scared to even breathe, let alone escape. I want them terrified, understand? Outta their mind. You think you can do that?"

Never scare her, the voice inside objected.

But shit, Monster was here for a reason. And he had to convince Bastian he could do the job. Otherwise, he wouldn't be here to see that his girl was okay. And the not knowing had been fucking killing him. He was this close, he wouldn't give up now.

So close to my Vegas. She was just beyond the door.

Monster smiled slow and vicious, letting Bastian see how it twisted his scars. He called on the darkest parts of him, needing to convince the asshole he was the man for the job. "I'll be their worst fucking nightmare."

And it worked, because Bastian nearly popped a hard-on at the promise of cruelty.

"Mmm, yes. I think you will." His hand went to the door handle and he twisted it. "You ready to meet my dolls?"

Monster's chest writhed with anticipation. He was going to see her. Put eyes on her. Just two more seconds...

His girl.

Fuck.

And then Bastian flung open the door, limping inside and clearing the way for Monster to follow.

Find her, find her...

The single bulb lamp gave only enough light to show him three terrified females. And none of them were his.

"Hello, dolls," Bastian rumbled low. "Meet your new nightmare. They call him *Monster*."

A shuffling under the bed caught his attention, and a small round face moved out of the shadow and into the light. Eyes so light they were gray stared at him, not looking away at the sight of his scars.

Her.

Her.

It started as a whisper.

And it would end with a bang.

******

Look for the next book in the

explosive Firecats series,

Heart of Glass,

coming this summer!

About the Author

P. Jameson likes to spend her time daydreaming, and then rearranging those dreams into heartstring-pulling stories of trial and triumph. Paranormal is her jam, so you're sure to find said stories full of hot alpha males of the supernatural variety. She lives next door to the great Rocky Mountains with her husband and kids, who provide her with plenty of writing fodder.

Made in the USA
Columbia, SC
19 October 2017